STICKS AND STONES

The greats in flash fiction

Edited by FJ Morris

Oxford Flash Fiction Prize

'Sticks and stones may break my bones.
But words can never hurt me.'

FROM THE EDITOR

Anyone who has ever heard the playground retort 'words can never hurt me' will know how absurd the phrase is. But whilst words have the power to hurt us, they also have the power to heal us.

These stories were written during one of the most difficult times we have experienced in decades. Months and years of isolation saw many people picking up a pen to connect with others. When we found ourselves physically cut off from the world, we also found that we could come together in other ways. The power of words saved many of us.

In 2020, after a few months of lockdown and recovering from the long-term effects of being one of the first to have COVID, I had an outrageous idea, and launched the Oxford Flash Fiction Prize. I had been writing flash fiction for years, and if it wasn't for competitions, I wouldn't be the writer I am today. Without them, I may not have finished anything at all. Each success was encouragement. Each milestone became more manageable, doable.

I launched the Oxford Flash Fiction Prize to inspire people to write. But the Oxford name is a double-edged sword. As someone who has come from a working-class neighbourhood, it was vital that this competition would go above and beyond in trying to level the playing field. Competitions and literary magazines are where most new writers begin. So, it is where they need to be encouraged the most, especially if they are from backgrounds that don't. I was determined to confront unconscious bias, to challenge the who-you-know culture, and dig deep into building foundations that would serve everyone who entered.

The response from writers, new and established, has blown me away:

Writer from Rajasthan, India, studying Sociology at Delhi University said: *'Honestly, in the pandemic things haven't been going great in life. Normal days also seem so challenging suddenly. Contests like the Oxford Flash Fiction Prize motivate me to read, write and be productive on days when I feel I just can't get up from the bed. However, as a student, I cannot enter contests with an entry fee. So when I found out that I got a free entry, I was beyond happy.'*

Nnadozie Onyekuru said: *'Entry or application fees, as modest as they seem, are often barriers for folks from low-income corners of the world. By providing such folks with free entries to its contest, the Oxford Flash Fiction Prize is removing barriers to participation and thus mitigating, in its little way, one subtle effect of global inequality.'*

Lydia Benson, new writer and second prize winner, said: *'I really appreciate the positivity in your emails. I loved when I entered that all the emails and the messages on the website were really encouraging. Since being long listed, I've felt really validated, so thank you!'*

A huge thank you goes to our readers, judges, critique team, administration team, and advisory committee, whose passion and skills have enabled the Prize to flourish. Thank you to all the authors in this anthology for sending us their incredible stories, and for everyone who entered and supported the competition.

But most of all, the biggest thank you goes to my partner. When I said I would like to set up a competition, his enthusiasm encouraged me to get started. Apparently, that was all I needed.

So, remember, words are powerful.

They can take you to places you never imagined.

I hope you enjoy where these stories take you.

--

Freya Morris
Director of the Oxford Flash Fiction Prize

CONTENTS

PART 1

*'We're united, you and I,
in holy antagonism, for as
long as we both shall live.'*

VIRUS

BY ROSE NEW

Well, hello there, human. Lovely to meet you. Lovely for me that is; not so much for you.

From my perspective, it's great to have found a host. It was a bit hairy for a moment there, floating around in the air, hitching a ride on a microscopic droplet.

I'd been inhabiting my last human for a few days already; so when I woke up from a little nap I thought: time to launch myself off on a new adventure. I crawled to the edge of the nasal passage and waited for a suitable exhalation – ideally a cough or a sneeze. Woah – there it was; actually a laugh – not quite as much momentum as a cough but it would have to do.

I am, of course, invisible. And with your limited imagination, you find it impossible to conceive of something you can't actually see. Look at the images you use of me – a many-headed, many-eyed sci-fi Medusa – a glowing sphere, sometimes orange, sometimes blue, pocked with bulbous protrusions. And that cute little emoji – vivid green, spouting delicate spikes like a dandelion clock.

In reality, I'm not so… charismatic.

Those few dizzying moments without a human to inhabit were exhilarating. What a voyage. You might think of me as Sir Walter Raleigh sailing to the New World, in search of riches to plunder. The ocean of air beat its waves. There was a window open somewhere;

I was buffeted on the currents. Picture me tugging desperately at the rigging, heaving the wheel.

You were just going about your business of existing, breathing. You didn't see the droplet galleon sailing towards you, with its crew of virus pirates. I threw a grappling hook and was on board. Clinging to your skin; appreciating its organic warmth.

You scratched your nose and I was in. Abseiling into your respiratory system. The triumph. I cackled to myself. Nothing could stop me now. Except your immune system, and that will take a while to kick in.

If I had ambition, wanted power and influence – what a triumph I would be celebrating now. Not just my own little victory, but the discord among humans. You blame, you condemn, you criticize. You report to the authorities or defy them. You cover your faces, as if ashamed. This is psychological warfare at its best. I might not have won glory on the battlefield, like say, bubonic plague, but as a biological terrorist, I'm uniquely successful.

So here we are, you and I, in our new relationship. You might think of this moment as a kind of wedding. You don't know it yet, in the veil of your ignorance. Your bouquet of vulnerability is so fragrant. The priest intones his blessing unheard. We're united, you and I, in holy antagonism, for as long as we both shall live. Tonight will be our wedding night. And yet, for now, you have no idea you're wearing my ring.

VIRUS BY ROSE NEW © 2021.

ROSE NEW IS A WRITER, TEACHER AND PARENT WHO LIVES IN MUDDY RURAL ESSEX, IN A HOUSE FILLED WITH THE BOOKS

OF HER ANCESTORS. SHE IS PASSIONATE ABOUT SHARING HER LOVE OF CREATIVE WRITING WITH STUDENTS. HER SHORT FICTION HAS BEEN PUBLISHED IN MAGAZINES AND ON WEBSITES, AND SHE HAS JUST COMPLETED A CHILDREN'S NOVEL.

STICKS AND STONES

BY ELIZABETH SMITH

THIRD PLACE WINNER

She spends every evening extricating words from where they've lodged beneath the surface of the skin. Most of the wounds are superficial and easily concealed. A few of the cuts are deeper and could probably do with a stitch or two, but she just sticks on a plaster and hopes that the blood won't seep through. She tells no one. The extracted words are shut in a box beneath the bed. They whisper to her at night.

Some words go straight in and out, like a needle. Others are barbed and get stuck, or splinter into shards. The Ms and the Ws are the worst. Fragments emerge – *inger, itch, hore* – and she has to poke around in the wound to find the missing letters. One night she extracts *man,* then pulls forth an *o* but the final *Bloody W* refuses to come. She puts the fragments she has removed, still coated in her blood, into the box. Eventually the skin closes over the rest of it, leaving a jagged scar which she conceals under long sleeves.

Occasionally someone will notice, even though the evidence is nearly always hidden. Her mum walks in on her, unannounced, after a particularly bad day, then phones the school. But this only makes it worse.

'They'll grow out of it you know, it won't last forever,' her mum tells her. As if she doesn't still have the scars from her own school days.

Her dad tells her to fight back, to arm herself with sticks and stones. What does he know? Her assailants are everywhere - the classroom, the corridors, her thoughts. Even under the watchful eye of the teacher they needle her. Sometimes the teacher joins in. She is a sitting target. She has tried feigning illness, lucky charms, and praying to God but her skin won't grow any thicker; the words still penetrate her soft, yielding flesh. All she can do is draw out the venom, letter by letter, word by word, and hope no infection takes hold.

One day a new girl appears and is placed at the desk next to hers.

'Look after Elaine, show her where everything is,' the teacher says.

She smiles shyly at the New Girl; the New Girl smiles shyly back.

At lunchtime she takes the New Girl to the canteen. The New Girl is quiet but, after a while, begins to chat more freely. The New Girl has moved around a lot and now lives only a few streets away. Can they walk home together? Anything she asks, the New Girl agrees.

But afterwards, the others are waiting. There are only five minutes before the bell and an extra two waiting for the teacher, who is late, but they work fast – surrounding the New Girl within seconds. Seven minutes is all they need. Later, when she asks a question, the New Girl pretends not to hear.

The New Girl comes to school the next day looking a bit less like herself and a bit more like them; swallowed up into the crowd of them at the start of the day and spat out at the gates. The New Girl never says anything hurtful, but the silence is nearly as bad.

And the words in the box grow, day by day. At night they come together - phrases become sentences, become paragraphs, become entire stories. Stories which narrate themselves. Stories she believes in.

Then, later, it could be weeks or months, it feels like years, she finds the New Girl waiting. It is as though they are back at day one. The New Girl follows her into the classroom, chatting about something she has done that weekend, as though they are friends. One of the others looks up as they enter, then returns to the huddle and says something which generates raucous laughter. The New Girl flushes deeply, and she thinks she sees the place the insult pierces before a sleeve is pulled down to hide it.

At lunchtime she prepares to make a quick getaway, as usual, when she feels a hand on her arm.

'Do you want to go to the canteen with me?' the New Girl asks.

Her reply shoots out like a dart, thrown wildly, before she has time to consider what she is saying.

'What, you think I want to go anywhere with you! Bitch!'

Then the New Girl is gone and she senses the heat of the others, feels the warmth from their smiles, as they absorb her.

Just like that, she is accepted. At lunchtime they take her in to town with them, during lessons she becomes the recipient of notes and gossip rather than the subject. One of them walks her to and from school. Her skin heals, the scars fade. She is invited to the cinema, parties, sleepovers – all she has ever imagined and more. All she has to do in return is sling more arrows; the deeper they penetrate, the greater the reward. She is good at it.

Her mum congratulates her.

'See? I told you it would work out.'

But she is not so sure. At night she lies awake, thinking of insults to use the next day. The words collide in her mind and make monsters. Shadows appear under her eyes. Her skin begins to itch and break out. No amount of make-up can hide it. She starts to miss school – pretending to be ill, or just not turning up. But she is soon caught and can think of no alternative but to continue.

One night, as she scratches in bed, she feels something hard beneath the skin. She turns on the light and faces herself in the full-length mirror. The itching intensifies. As she watches, the old wounds reopen like hungry, gaping mouths. Something dark and jagged emerges from freshly parted flesh. She takes it and automatically reaches for the box. Inside, the words lie silent and glistening. One by one, she begins to insert them into her skin.

STICKS AND STONES BY ELIZABETH SMITH © 2021.

ELIZABETH SMITH IS A FULL-TIME MOTHER AND OCCASIONAL WRITER. HER POETRY HAS BEEN PUBLISHED IN FIREWORDS MAGAZINE. WHEN SHE'S NOT CHASING AFTER HER TWO YOUNG CHILDREN SHE ENJOYS READING, RUNNING AND DAYDREAMING. SHE CURRENTLY LIVES IN SCOTLAND.

SKIN

BY DANIEL DRAPER

SECOND PLACE WINNER

She was born with a caul, but at least she was human. At the birth I shut my eyes, terrified. The metallic smell of blood mixed with brine and earth under Sandra's screams and I only opened them once I heard the midwife's surprise. It was a surprise without horror. I'd never seen a caul before. It wrapped around her tiny head like a giant extra eyelid. If we rushed, our baby's skin would peel off with it. The midwife sliced at the nostrils so our girl could breath and little white ridges of extra skin bunched together over her hair. I looked at Sandra. I thought, if she panics, you can panic. I had questions that were too personal to ask, even though I'd witnessed the birth. Sandra's face was distant, reminding me of a church statue above salvation's doors. She had blanched eyes, and her mouth was turned downwards, as if mourning. I'd never been happier.

The midwife cooed and gasped at the rarity of it, congratulating us like a judge on a baking show, marvelling at what we could rustle up given such unique ingredients. Roman lawyers would buy stolen cauls for luck, she said, joking that we should sell it. Neither of us laughed. Sandra gently held our miracle in one arm and in the other caressed the sleeve with its small slit, the only thing stopping our daughter from suffocating before she had a chance to open her eyes.

When the midwife insisted we keep it for posterity, Sandra's eyes refocused, glistening as they met our daughters'. They were the same deep chestnut, and just as wet. Her newly uncovered cheeks were so full they threatened to evict her nose. Sandra told the midwife to get rid of it and I exhaled, unaware I'd been holding my breath.

We were married two summers ago. The wedding had been family only, taking place in the shallow lapping of the coast. It was sunset, long after the fishermen had gone home. She wore a sheer white dress and had shells in her salted hair, while I was wearing the tweed jacket that I'd tried on in a charity shop to make her laugh. We'd giggled amongst other people's castoffs and I told her I loved her for the first time.

Her brothers and mother had stepped out of their skins completely, pale and naked against the rocks, standing knee deep in the water. My mother had deemed it a power move on their part, which she matched with a hat that you could have set sail in. My brother officiated and we celebrated with a picnic on the rocks, my new in-laws doing their best to answer questions about life underwater as my family tried to explain what weddings meant to humans. Our fathers refused to come, their opposition being the only thing they had in common.

Sandra said they had always found the skin restrictive, but it was the only thing that would keep them warm in the depths. She didn't like to talk about things from before us, and I certainly couldn't visit, but every time she went I felt the goodbye pinch in my throat. What if she decided to stay? I could have hidden the skin, but that felt too cruel. We keep it preserved in seawater, by my surfing stuff in the garage.

We had no idea how pregnancy would work, and there was no chance of asking the doctor, but things were good. The inside of her changed as I had nightmares of baby seals screaming. I knew there were bones and a little heart in there as I lay my hand on her belly at night, but I couldn't stop thinking about the skin. The outside on the inside. Skin within skin under skin.

We brought her home and named her, and life went on. Sometimes I come home and Sandra is in the garage with the skin in her arms, the baby beside her. There's a soft grief in the way she tells her stories that I can't bear, so I leave them to it. She didn't tell her parents about the baby. She said it was cruel to dangle a grandchild just out of their reach, even though I'd always said they were welcome to visit, particularly in the cold winters. Apparently I didn't understand.

I tried to be romantic and booked a day off work without telling her. I made her breakfast and brought it to her in bed with the skin. I'll take care of the baby, I told her, you go visit your folks for the day. Her head fell and she started a low hum that broke into a wail. I didn't know what I'd done and she couldn't stop screaming long enough to tell me. I took myself over to the moses basket, not wanting to panic the little one. She wiggled in my arms but stayed silent, listening to her mother's heart breaking. I spent the day holding them both, alternating as needed, and fell asleep between them in exhaustion.

It was dark when Sandra woke me up. She was feeding the baby, her soft crying worse than the wailing. She told me her skin didn't fit anymore. She couldn't go back into the sea. She couldn't feel currents and whirls of darkness surround her, and she couldn't say goodbye to her mother or introduce our daughter.

She'd been telling the stories as lullabies, watching pudgy fingers try to grasp the skin, instinctively placing it over her tiny head. We'll save the skin, I said, and when she was old enough, she could take it. Visit. Explain. It was fixable.

Before Sandra could explain why I was wrong, our daughter unlatched and gave us a gurgled smile as she slipped between waking and sleeping. Sandra beamed, and in my throat a hiccough of love bubbled and burst with such force that for a moment I was convinced I was drowning.

SKIN BY DANIEL DRAPER © 2021.

DANIEL DRAPER IS A PRIZE-WINNING WRITER FROM DERBYSHIRE WHOSE WORK IS INFLUENCED BY THE UNCANNY AND MACABRE OF THE EVERYDAY. IF HE ISN'T WRITING OR TEACHING, HE'S PROBABLY ON TWITTER @MRDRAPERMATHS.

READY THE HEART

BY LYNSEY MAY

COMPETITION FINALIST

Thursday, it was lungs. The month before we had eyes. Well, corneas if you want to get technical, which I never do and Stuart always does. Fussing over the nitty gritty helps him. I prefer the big picture. Sloppy strokes too, where it's easier to find a little swipe of magic.

We're getting ready for the heart. I'm not going to lie, it's the one I've been waiting for.

I couldn't sleep last night. I'm not much of a sleeper, these days. Stuart snuffled his way into dreams as I lay still enough to hear. I know it's my blood pressure and anxiety and the dark silence of the night that does it, but it felt special this time.

I got up early and made myself a coffee. Stuart prefers tea and I do too, but Paulie drank coffee and every now and then I like to make myself one using that machine of his. It's so bulky and black, it looks all wrong in the kitchen but now it's here I can't imagine the counter without it.

I'm jittery. I blame it on the wrong kind of caffeine and Stuart only raises an eyebrow. I button my good blouse and wait for him to go and brush his teeth. He looks as tired as I feel but I know he's excited too.

He programmes the address into his phone's map. We let them choose the place. It's a little clue for us and a comfort for them. We're off to a Chinese buffet place today. A chain.

We don't talk on the drive there and that's fine. We arrive early, we always do, and I hook a nice, bright yellow umbrella on the back of my chair before I sit down. I can't be the one walking in, scanning a room full of diners for the right face. This is the routine and it's worked well. Stuart doesn't like it, but not so much that he'll try and change it.

A plate piled with starters is carried by and I remember when Paulie realised that paper wrapped prawns had actual prawns in them. He thought... I don't know what he thought. That they were made of paper? The newly formed connection between creatures and flesh horrified him. Those sad parcels stiffened on the side of his plate, pale prawn chunks growing pinker.

He got over it. Went through a phase where meat was all he wanted. He relished anything on the bone, tore at it like a little king, grease smeared from cheek to chin. I grinned and bore it, waiting for the next phase. Who knew he'd end up rhapsodizing over pho, sous vide cooked steaks and always, always a black coffee.

And so we sit. A big man enters the restaurant. A really big man, almost a foot taller than Paulie and a good bit wider. His brows are scrunched and his mouth pursed. I look down, hoping it's not him.

It is him.

He walks over and says our names, softly. I jump up and we hover until Stuart says, nice to meet you and we take it as a signal to sit down. I tell him it means a lot to us, him coming. He shakes his head, a little flush of red showing at the collar of his shirt.

Stuart asks if this is a favourite spot of his and the

man offers up another little shake. He's too smart to meet us somewhere he wouldn't be willing to give up. I'm glad. He stares at the menu like it's a script.

Stuart and I won't be able to eat a bite, we never can. The man doesn't look like much will put him off his food. Or maybe I'm not being unfair and it's just the pills.

Did you, I start. Are you... I can't go on. Normally, I do all the talking. I have always been good at filling silences. Except today, in amongst all the clinks of forks of ceramic and the snap of cheap disposable chopsticks and people discussing what they will eat and what they'll do next and whether they should leave a tip, my ears fill.

The man is looking at me. There is nothing of Paulie in him. There's been none of Paulie in any of them. I stared into those corneas last month hoping for just the tiniest flicker and I am not a stupid woman, I know that's not how it works. It didn't stop me staring.

Now, I try to smile at this big man we know nothing about. Who we're here to find out about. And it comes to me that it doesn't matter what we hear, it's not going to be enough. Each of these people with a little piece of Paulie in them is never going to be enough. They'll never be what I want. I don't know what we've been doing all these months.

I am going to shoot into the sky, implode, fall to pieces, embarrass my poor husband and this utter stranger in a soulless buffet place we never should have come to. I stand, my chair tips back. The man reaches out to right it and then he is holding me tight. He is so much bigger than Stuart, than Paulie, that even though I am old enough to be his mother, I feel a comfort that stretches back to my youngest days.

Gently but firmly, he presses my head to his chest, my ear to his heart, and there it is, the slow, steady thump that once belonged to my son.

Paulie is gone and I don't have to be grateful for the good his parts are doing. It is enough that they existed in one form and now they are another. It has to be enough that he existed.

I cry into the stranger's musty shirt. I've heard all I needed to hear.

READY THE HEART BY LYNSEY MAY © 2021.

LYNSEY MAY LIVES, LOVES AND WRITES IN EDINBURGH. HER SHORT FICTION HAS BEEN PUBLISHED IN VARIOUS JOURNALS AND ANTHOLOGIES, INCLUDING THE STINGING FLY, GUTTER AND BANSHEE. SHE'S NEVER FAR FROM A CUP OF COFFEE AND HER BAG IS ALWAYS TOO HEAVY.

MY BROKEN NOSE

BY SIMON HARRIS

Getting my nose broken at a very early stage in my professional career has undoubtedly been the single most important learning experience I've ever had as a journalist. It has taught me a key lesson that I've carried with me to disaster sites and war zones all over the world.

We all know that those 'who', 'what', 'where', 'when', 'why' and 'how' questions are fundamentally important, but in a critical context they can be even more laden with sensitivities than usual. Basically, if you don't know *who* to interview and *who* to leave alone; or *what* question to ask first and *what* not to ask; or you have no sense of timing about *when* or even *where* to ask your questions – then you just might end up getting your nose broken like I did.

I am sure you all want to know how it happened, don't you? Well, the short answer is this: a vicious sledgehammer blow from the angry fist of a Welsh miner! But of course, that only invites more questions, so I guess I will have to tell you the whole story.

I was eighteen, had just finished school and managed to get a job down in Swansea as a cub reporter for the *Evening Post*. They had put me on the obituary column. When word of the landslide first came in, I was at my typewriter trying to work out something to say about some old rugby star from the last century who had died the previous day. I could see the editor in his glass-panelled office giving animated instructions to one of the newspapers' senior correspondents and a photographer. Suddenly he turned to point at me and flung open the door.

'You boy! You're from up in the Valleys, aren't you?'

'Yes sir.'

'Know where Aberfan is then?'

'Yes sir.'

'Got yourself a driver's license, have you?'

'Yes sir.'

'Right then,' he said to the other two as he flung me a set of car keys, 'that's your driver sorted!'

By the time we got to Aberfan the road into the village had been blocked by the police who were only letting emergency vehicles through. As my colleagues got off to walk, leaving me to park the car in a farmers' field, I asked them what I should do.

'You're a reporter, aren't you son?'

I nodded.

'Then take your pad and pen, ask some questions and write a story, it's as simple as that.'

Minutes later I had parked the car, run down the lane after them and was in the village. Although I've since got used to such sights over the years, the shock of that first time has never left me. Not the destruction and piles of rubble. Not the covered row of tiny bodies laid out on the floor of the chapel. It was the faces of the people, almost void of hope and yet somehow still clinging on amidst a dawning realisation of the desolation around them.

In a daze, I stumbled across the black debris until I came face to face with a man, spade in hand, stripped

19

down to his vest and covered in so much dust that the only white remaining was that surrounding the pupils of his wild eyes. He stared blankly at me for a few long seconds before turning back to wedge his spade behind a large stone.

As he strained to lever it free, I cleared my throat and tapped him on the shoulder. 'Excuse me sir, would you mind if I asked you a couple of questions?'

All I remember before losing consciousness was the sound of my nose cracking and a man's voice booming over me.

'AND WOULD *YOU* MIND IF I FOUND MY BOYS FIRST?'

MY BROKEN NOSE BY SIMON HARRIS © 2021.

SIMON HARRIS IS BRITISH AND LIVES IN SRI LANKA. HIS STORIES HAVE APPEARED IN FLASH, THE SHORT-SHORT STORY MAGAZINE, FLASH FICTION MAGAZINE, CRANNOG MAGAZINE AND THE HUFFINGTON POST.

CONVALESCENCE

BY MATTHEW TUCKER

COMPETITION FINALIST

'It's not as bad as you imagine, it never is,' Corporal Goddard said as he combed the soldier's hair. The dark strands parted easily, oiled by sweat and grease. The soldier lay still, letting his hair be groomed. 'You've had quite a tumble,' he added.

The patient said nothing. It was three weeks since Goddard had been assigned nurse duties in the small field hospital. He was getting used to the heavy silence of traumatised men.

'People can feel like they've lost half their face, even when their face is still all there: nose, eyes...' he said. 'I promise you: your mother could still pick you out of a line-up of rogues.'

'Show me a mirror then,' the soldier said suddenly, meeting his eyes for the first time.

He shook his head. 'That's not a good idea. Not this early. Besides, we don't have hand mirrors to give out.'

The soldier stared ahead at the brown canvas wall. 'Bullshit.'

Goddard stopped moving his hand and laid the comb to rest. The dark hair was as neat as a ploughed field of earth. He looked behind him and across the line of sleeping men to a desk where two superiors sat puffing on their pipes, examining papers.

'You're welcome to search the storeroom for mirrors,' he said, turning back to the patient, 'but I think you'd be restrained sharpish. The Big Nurse here: he has arms the size of ham joints, and tattoos that'd make you blush.'

The patient gave a snort and closed his eyes.

'My girl said she liked my dimples best...' the soldier said. 'She spotted me from across a crowded pub because of 'em. The dimples called to her, she said. Well, I ain't got fucking dimples now.'

The man's voice lacked colour. It was like he was speaking in black and white, like the daily newsreels with the sound turned down. Goddard picked up the comb again, then rested his hand on the man's pillow.

'You aren't as pretty as an oil painting, I'll give you that. But girls love war wounds. Germans get surgeons to cut their cheeks to give them scars, just to get the girls to look twice.'

The soldier opened his eyes. 'I ain't no German.'

Goddard put the comb in his pocket and pulled up a wooden chair. He sat down and leaned close to the man's head.

'Listen, I have an idea...' he said, lowering his voice. 'I like to draw. Would you let me sketch you? It'll be as good as a mirror, better even; you'll be able to send the picture back to your girl.'

The soldier looked up shyly.

'And I'll put the dimples in,' Goddard added, 'even if it's poetic licence.'

'Poetic what?'

'Like when you bend the truth, just a little, to put things in the best possible light.'

The soldier opened his eyes a little wider. Goddard

22

saw they were green. 'So you won't draw me with this bandage around my head?'

'Not if you don't want me to.'

The man licked his lips. 'Best not. She'll worry herself into the ground if she sees it.' He started trying to sit up, pushing through the dulled pain. Goddard stepped to the next empty bed and brought over a pillow, wedging it under the man's head so that he settled into a half seated and half slumped position with his neck supported by the extra padding. He went to a battered locker at the far end of the makeshift ward and returned with a thin sketchpad and short pencil.

The patient was trying to rearrange the hair sprouting from the wrapping around his head, his thumb and index finger grasping at the black fringe. The rest of his fingers were tied together in a tight splint and waved in the air like a wounded flipper. 'No need, I've seen to that,' Goddard said, gently easing the man's hand down to the blanket, 'it's as glossy as a horse's mane.'

He sat down and hunched forward over his pad. He gripped the stubby pencil between his fingers under his chin, like a skinny recreation of Rodin's The Thinker.

'Imagine what your girl will say when she gets a portrait. She'll think you're a hero of the trenches. Have you been going steady for long?'

The patient gave a proud nod. 'Since we were sixteen.'

Goddard surveyed the young face like a canvas. 'I'll draw you how she sees you: fearless.'

He ignored the dark scabs that were starting to peel off the soldier's nose and lips, and the stains of yellow and purple flesh around his cheekbones, looking tender like spoilt fruit. He didn't look at the hollow near his jawbone, a wound that would heal to be a moon crater on his face.

He searched for the skin between the damage; tanned and smooth. Goddard put the pencil to paper and started to sketch the eyes.

MATTHEW TUCKER RECENTLY COMPLETED A GOTHIC NOVELLA AND IS WORKING ON A NOVEL THAT IS SPECULATIVE FICTION ABOUT CLIMATE CHANGE. HE COMPLETED A BA DEGREE IN ENGLISH LITERATURE AND CREATIVE WRITING AT BANGOR UNIVERSITY IN NORTH WALES, WHERE HE ENJOYED TRYING HIS HAND AT FICTION, POETRY AND SCREENWRITING. HE WENT ON TO TRAIN AS A JOURNALIST, WORKING FOR THE HUFFINGTON POST UK AND BUZZFEED UK. HE'S CURRENTLY A PICTURE PRODUCER FOR BBC NEWS ONLINE & MOBILE, AND LIVES NEXT TO THE THAMES IN GREENWICH BOROUGH, LONDON.

TOUCH ME AGAIN BEFORE I DIE

BY DAVID LEWIS

William had the touch of an angel. He spoilt me for everyone else.

I'd been shipped from Yokohama and reassembled in a London showroom. William had failed to become a concert pianist and was working as a tuner. He had long hair, torn jeans and a T-shirt with a faded print of Arthur Rubinstein. Approaching me with respect, adjusting the stool with care, he roused me gently with scales and arpeggios in every key, major and minor. After twiddling under my lid, propped open as high as possible, he rippled up and down from my lowest A to highest C, smoothly and with syncopation, at increasing speed. And then he brought me to climax with the Brahms Rhapsody in G minor, Opus 79 No. 2. I have never resonated like that again.

A rich couple brought their son into the showroom. 'His teacher says he's ready to upgrade,' the mother simpered to the salesman, who was keen to promote the pricier Bechstein next to me. 'Only the best is good enough for Benjamin.'

I'm the best piano, of course — I am a Kawai, after all — and the spoilt brat chose me. Not because of my superb touch or depth of tone, though, but because he preferred the shape of my music rack. Benjamin's father backed his son's choice, relieved to pay several thousands pounds less than he'd feared.

They installed me in their fancy house at the disposal and mercy of Benjamin. Though not totally unmusical, the boy was appallingly lazy. He preferred to play *Für Elise* repeatedly than to practise new pieces that would have lit my fire, made me glow, let me sing. After a Robert Redford film made Scott Joplin all the rage, Benjamin would bang out *The Entertainer* over and over until he drove me mad. I ask you! Rags are for out-of-tune pub pianos, not pedigree instruments like me. And then Benjamin's younger sister began lessons; I had to endure being under-used and abused with *Twenty Tunes for Tiny Tots.*

Things got even worse after both kids gave up the piano. I became a glorified mantelpiece for vases, photos and plants. Somewhere for guests to deposit their glasses and canapés during cocktail parties. Or for visiting children to play chop-sticks with sticky fingers, scratch initials on my fine lacquer, or spill Coca Cola into my guts. Now the children have left home, I am to be sold. I've only ever wanted to serve. To look and sound beautiful. To let my shiny body reveal all its secrets and richness by being touched, caressed and pounded by a master. To take my listeners to heaven and back, in poignancy and thunder.

The showroom is sending someone to examine me for re-sale. Someone who will take me apart, remove the coins jammed between my keys and replace my damaged felts. Someone who will tickle my ivories again.

I hope that someone will be William.

DAVID LEWIS HAS WORKED AS A FOREIGN CORRESPONDENT, WRITER ON AIDS FOR WHO, AND SPOKESMAN FOR THE EUROPEAN BROADCASTING UNION. HE NOW LIVES AND WRITES IN FERNEY-VOLTAIRE, NEAR FRANCE'S BORDER WITH SWITZERLAND. HIS EARLY COLLECTION OF SONNETS WON A PRIZE AT CAMBRIDGE UNIVERSITY. SEVERAL STAGE PIECES HAVE BEEN PREMIÈRED IN GENEVA AND PUBLISHED IN THE ANNUAL LITERARY REVIEW EX TEMPORE. THE FIRST CHAPTERS OF HIS THIRD NOVEL, MADE IN HUNGARY, WERE PUBLISHED BY PANORAMA JOURNAL AND NOMINATED FOR A PUSHCART PRIZE. HE HAS BECOME A KEEN FLASHER SINCE JOINING THE RETREAT WEST COMMUNITY. IN 2021 HE WON THE BANGOR 40 WORDS COMPETITION FOR MICRO-FICTION.

TWO SUGARS

BY AUDREY NIVEN

From under your hand's salute, you look into the sun. It tastes of salmon paste and lemonade. The thermos is taken from the back of the press and steeped for two days with baking soda. Tiny bubbles lift the ghosts, until it is fresh as a Livingstone daisy.

Outwardly all is colourful. Limbs unfurl like the time-lapsed tendrils of ferns, and summer clothes blossom in gardens and parks. Bare feet run on soft grass, bare shoulders thrill to the breeze.

Strong hands unscrew two layers of cups, one with a handle, one without. They grip the flask by the neck and twist at its most vulnerable point. Ice-cream bells chime in the distance. The pressure is released.

A game of rounders is under way, all in it for the fun and no care to winning. Legs grow tanned as the summer moves through the game. The hand that holds the larger cup has a swallow tattoo and doesn't bother with the handle.

'Two,' he says, not looking up when sugar is offered, spooned into the cup and stirred with care, mindful not to splash hot tea over the side. His eyes are felt, burning, on thighs as they run back to the stump. They travel up and down again: ear, clavicle, nipple, hip, knee, ankle. The skin feels the eyes, feels the betrayal, too hot for camomile lotion to soothe.

You bite into a cone as he touches you, cauterising the wound with sugar and cold. You let the sun blind you, bleaching away the moment with light as you wait for it to pass. When the clouds come over, the thermos is put away for another year, its delicate silvery innards protected by a vacuum of silence. The swallow has long since flown, but the scald will never cool.

AUDREY NIVEN IS A SCOTTISH WRITER, LIVING IN LONDON. HER FLASH FICTION HAS APPEARED IN MULTIPLE ANTHOLOGIES AND ON-LINE JOURNALS INCLUDING THE BATH FLASH FICTION ANTHOLOGY, NATIONAL FLASH FICTION DAY, REFLEX PRESS, LUNATE FICTION, EL-LIPSISZINE, 101 WORDS, AND SECOND CHANCE LIT. @NIVENAUDREY

FOR THE LOVE OF PLANTAINS

BY CORNERLIS KWEKU AFFRE

I was distraught. It was seven days to the festival of Harvests and someone had stolen my choicest plantains. Those were to be presented to Aku's family as a token of my love for her and to finally ask for her hand in marriage.

I was just one of about 20 suitors who had made known their intention to pursue the beautiful Aku as their wife.

Others were presenting fish, yams, eggs, oranges and cow legs; but I knew what Aku loved most – plantains. She loved them ripe, yellow and soft – so soft they melt on the tongue.

My heart was troubled. No matter what happens Aku would make a choice in seven days.

It was then you announced your arrival. You, Koao, were to meet me at the riverside when the sky was only turning orange. But the sky was bleeding red now. 'I was busy,' you said. You had been helping your mother on her farm, you said. 'Forgive me. I won't be late again,' you told me, for the hundredth time.

You pulled out something wrapped in plantain leaves from your raffia satchel. It was kaaklo, cold from being in that satchel for too long.

'Here, take, a peace offering.' You handed the kaaklo to me and asked, 'What's up? What's the matter?' I took a bite from the delicious kaaklo, and I told you about the theft on my farm.

I told you if I don't see my plantains in seven days, my dream of marrying Aku would be drowned in the Bio River never to surface again. I told you that would be the end of me and I could possibly die from heartbreak.

You listened attentively, punctuating my monologue with sighs and groans. You seemed to share in my pain. 'You will find the culprit. We will get the plantains and you will marry Aku,' you assured.

But where were we going to start? You told me to leave it to you and gave me more kaaklo.

The day after, I heard no news from you. My plantains had not returned. And more suitors were presenting gifts to Aku.

According to Kyei, the gong beater, Moro the skinny Dagati boy had dragged a bull by its horns to Aku's house. Her brothers were impressed. I hear she even smiled at him. But I know my plantains would have done more than that.

The next day you came to my house. 'I have a lead!' you said.

I ended up beating Danso, the town drunkard, Mensah, Agya Nimo's last born, Kusi the poor hunter, and Xorlali, the boy who eats everything with okro stew. For days you led me on a wild goose chase beating the sense out of innocent men and still my plantains weren't in sight.

Soon it was a day to when Aku decides and I hadn't found my plantains. I was furious. If my strength wouldn't do the trick then the gods would.

I was going to summon the thief to Faakye to exact judgment. But you said no. 'You know it's a grave offence to pronounce a curse to Faakye. The King might have your head,' you said, blocking the path to Faakye's shrine.

I had heard enough. 'I am going. If I can't have her, that thief wouldn't too.'

You dropped to your knees and held me rooted to the ground. 'If the king takes your head, I'll have no friend. Please don't do this.'

So I stayed. And you stayed with me - the whole day. You followed me everywhere, leading me everywhere, but to Faakye's grove. You stayed until the sun retired and the moon took over. Save for your mother sending your little sister to come fetch you, you'd have slept in my hut with me.

Immediately after you left, I sped to Faakye's grove. Death must visit anyone who had touched my plantains. Bloody rageful death.

On the seventh day, I was sitting atop a neem tree facing Aku's compound when I saw your cousin, Kobina, flanked by his mother and yours, with you following behind carrying my plantains in a basin big enough to bathe you in, headed towards Aku's compound.

You were anxious. You were looking around to see if you would spot me first. But I had seen your treachery. I couldn't stay to watch. I went to Bio.

You came to the riverside to look for me only after Aku had accepted the plantains. Only after she had smiled and whispered 'yes' in her mother's ears as a response to your cousin's proposal. Only after a wedding date had been set for their marriage.

You knew I had found out the truth. 'I can explain,' you pleaded. You had stolen the plantains and given them to your cousin as payment for a debt your family owed his.

For the secret to Aku's heart, all that you owed would be forgiven, and that promise was the knife with which you stabbed me in the back.

I was furious. Was this how you were going to repay me for all the times I had your back? For all the times I had been more than a friend to you? You were a betrayer, a traitor and only your blood flowing like the Bio was going to pacify my anger.

I smashed your head with a rock I was palming. You landed in the water, your head bleeding. You tried escaping. But I was swifter and stronger. I trapped you between my legs and squeezed your neck while drowning you.

Before long your thrashing in the water had stopped. Your body, limp and your eyes, lifeless. You were dead. A bloody rageful death.

'What have I done?' I thought. But it was too late now. I could see evil eyes of demons peering back at me from behind the woods. I was next. The kaaklo you had offered me was one of mine after all.

FOR THE LOVE OF PLANTAINS BY CORNERLIS KWEKU AFFRE © 2021.

CORNERLIS KWEKU AFFRE IS A FINAL YEAR STUDENT OF THE GHANA INSTITUTE OF JOURNALISM, MAJORING IN JOURNALISM. HE'S 21 YEARS OLD AND RESIDES IN GHANA. HE HAS A PASSION FOR STORYTELLING, AND BELIEVES A FAIR AND APPROPRIATE REPRESENTATION OF PEOPLE, ESPECIALLY MINORITY GROUPS IN THE GHANAIAN MEDIA LANDSCAPE, WOULD GO A LONG WAY TO ERADICATE THE PHOBIA AND PUBLIC RIDICULE THEY'RE FORCED TO ENDURE. HE DOES NOT CONFORM TO A SINGLE LITERARY

GENRE AS HE BELIEVES THE AFRICAN STORY NEEDS TO BE TOLD IN AS MANY DIVERSE WAYS AS POSSIBLE. HE ASPIRES TO BE A FILMMAKER, A TRAVELER, A WEALTHY MAN AND AN AUTHOR. HE HAS BEEN PUBLISHED IN DRAMA QUEENS' 2019 CULTURAL ZINE, AND HIS STORY - AT THE ALTAR - TOUCHED ON PUBLIC HATE, AND THE CRUEL TREATMENT OF LGBTQ PEOPLE ON THE CONTINENT.

EVERY TIME I SMELL PINEAPPLE GRILLING

BY BRITTANY TERWILLIGER

COMPETITION FINALIST

I plonk the cream carton next to my empty mug while the coffee drips, then remember I'm alone and take a big swig straight from the cardboard lip. If she was here, she wouldn't get mad at me, she'd take the carton from my hand and take a big swig, too.

❖ ❖ ❖

A man approaches us on the tennis court, empty on a Tuesday morning, and asks to take our picture for the local paper. My mom smiles at him but goes rigid, asks me to come closer to her. To my eight-year-old heart this is a jackpot, getting singled out—selected —for doing nothing extraordinary at all, and I can't understand why my mom isn't ecstatic. Why she locks us both in the car as soon as he leaves, and takes the long way home.

❖ ❖ ❖

My sister calls to say Mom passed out watching the kids again, red Solo cup still half full of vodka. She says the kids didn't even notice this time, they were in the other room tearing all the windows out of the doll-house. She says this one was the last straw though, because when she tried waking Mom up, she didn't move. 'I really thought she was dead,' my sister says. I think what she means is she wants the kids to remember their grandma the way we remember her.

◆ ◆ ◆

I click the thingy next to the temperature dial, but nothing happens. I can smell the propane, see its clear waves rising toward the sun. Mom is in the air conditioning, showing my best friend Andrea how to baste the pineapple with teriyaki sauce. 'Use a match,' she yells through the screen door. I toss a lit match in and nothing happens. Then, as I lean my face closer, *bloof*, the grill blows a fireball 8 feet in the air. I hear my mom's abundant laugh. 'Still have your eyebrows?' she shouts.

◆ ◆ ◆

I answer the phone and my mom, all deadtone and slurred speech, says that she cut herself last week but didn't go deep enough. 'I just thought you should know,' she says. Sometimes I wonder if she even loves me. How could she love anyone if she's willing to do this to herself? I say the only thing I can think of: we've all been there, it'll get better. But it's a lie, I haven't been there, and it isn't getting any fucking better. I call my sister, 'go check on Mom, she's hitting the sauce,' and we huff and sigh, and I wonder if maybe we all like the drama a little too much. Maybe we all need someone to blame.

◆ ◆ ◆

We've opened our presents and my grandpa is stepping between us, picking up wads of paper and stuffing them in a trash bag. Mom says she's got one more, and quietly giggles as she pulls the envelope out of her purse. My sister and I are already twisting the plastic ties from the backs of our new Barbie boxes, and Mom shushes us, tells us to pay attention. Granny has this pasted-on smile, like she knows she's supposed to be excited and this is the best she can do. She slides her index finger through the envelope, which the rest of us already know is a gift certificate for a home cleaning service. Granny hates to clean, so we are expecting one of those weighty, teary-eyed thank yous, the kind that understands how much time and thought and care went into choosing this thing just for you. But Granny studies the certificate with a stony expression, then says 'I don't want someone coming in my house' and tosses the envelope on the floor. Head down, my mom puts it back in her purse, and says sorry she has to go to the bathroom.

❖ ❖ ❖

I call the hotline and the woman's kindness feels like a stifling, sweaty room. I hear my voice turn cold and clipped. Just tell me how to get my mother into rehab, I don't want your goddamned sympathy. Thinking of her later, I imagine the woman's big arms pulling me into a hug, and I sit on the floor with a dish towel over my face and shake out reservoirs of grief that seem to multiply the moment I touch them.

❖ ❖ ❖

In my dream, we are riding bikes. Mine has training

wheels, and my sister is in the kiddie seat on the back of our mom's old ten-speed. Everywhere there is wide-open grassy space. More space than the mind can fathom. So much space it feels like I could take off and fly.

EVERY TIME I SMELL PINEAPPLE GRILLING BY BRITTANY TERWILLIGER © 2021.

BRITTANY TERWILLIGER IS MANAGING EDITOR AT PITHEAD CHAPEL AND HER NOVEL, THE INSATIABLES (CHICAGO REVIEW PRESS) WAS PUBLISHED IN 2018. HER SHORT FICTION HAS APPEARED IN JMWW, (MAC)RO(MIC), GHOST PARACHUTE, FIVE:2:ONE, PONDER REVIEW, ELLIPSIS ZINE, AND ELSEWHERE, AND HAS BEEN NOMINATED FOR BEST OF THE NET, BEST MICROFICTION, AND THE PUSHCART PRIZE. FIND HER ON TWITTER @BRTTNYBLM.

MORNINGS WERE FOR MILK

BY JENN MURRAY

We ran away together. The boy from Trouble and I from Music. He stole his neighbors Ford Mustang, cream with a red line through the center. I took my Mother's cello. Sweat laden forearms hung out the window, driving for highway days. Salty kisses on picnic benches turned into weak coffee at dusk.

We positioned ourselves in maid's quarters off a farm. He cooked grits and eggs and I played low notes to replace the breeze hiding in late September.

Mornings were for milk. Lady Denver let us take our share from a cow going spare. She told me more than him not to come knocking.

I crossed the sun-kissed wheat field early in my white nightgown. The smell of hay and shit ran against each other inside the barn, but the shadows were nice on my shoulders.

Something called from the back. Antlers first, peering over the last stall. Oak's naked branches. I'm a magnet for Winter friends. His eyes were golden and his body dormant. When he shook his head, bells sang in a secret.

'Blitzen.'

A first-class voice at the entrance. Lady Denver's man. Waistcoat and a pocket watch glinting at me.

'I'm Silver,' I said, standing with my bucket of breakfast.

'I know.' Man looked over my shoulder. 'Nick leaves Blitzen here over the summer.'

'Nick?' But wealth was gone. The reindeer pouted his lips, looking for a kiss. My hand found his head and I caressed. I walked back to Trouble's son, withholding.

'Stop singing,' he said through the shower curtain. He added less butter to my dinner, sniffing a betrayal.

I abandoned the cello. Serenading was lying. Our romance got lost in the empty money jar. Blitzen and I practiced at dawn, when the boy dreamt of answers. His hooves tired at first but soon, a feathery delight. After a fortnight, we could float. I went over the top of him twice when he landed, the antlers ripping my cotton dress. I took it off at the doorway calling for loving in case Trouble's son thought I was fooling around with the Denver man.

'We'll get rich, baby,' said his overheated apology in my ear.

I wanted to work for Nick. Earn coins that glint. He'd dress me in fur because the storybooks say it's cold up north. I'd make presents for the little ones who were hopeful enough to write a letter. I never did. Mother Music blocked the chimney.

When morning still looked like night, I pulled on overalls discarded in the bedroom corner and crept outdoors. Lady Denver's boots rested on the doorstep drying out from the midnight rain. I laced them around my bare ankles.

In the barn I climbed onto his back, grabbing the

short neck hair and we meandered out to the field. 'Can I go with you?' I whispered. 'Let's leave Summer.'

He cantered. We flew. Too high to go back. The cream of the car roof merged into the wheat as the sun climbed its ladder.

JENN MURRAY IS AN ACTRESS AND WRITER FROM BELFAST, LIVING AND WORKING IN NEW YORK CITY. HER MORE RECENT FILM CREDITS INCLUDE MALEFICENT 2 WHERE SHE PLAYED THE VILLAIN GERDA OPPOSITE ANGELINA JOLIE AND MICHELLE PFIEFFER, LOVE AND FRIENDSHIP AND BROOKLYN. JJ ABRAMS AWARDED HER THE OSCAR WILDE AWARD IN HOLLYWOOD IN FEBRUARY 2020. HER SHORT STORY 'THE BLUE DRESS' WAS LONG LISTED IN AUGUST FOR REFLEX FLASH FICTION PRIZE. HER FIRST NOVEL - ROCK PAPER SCISSORS - IS CURRENTLY BEING REVIEWED BY LITERARY AGENTS.

PART 2

'I know the dog and the dog knows me. I might even give it a name. Or would they think I'm mad?'

TWENTY-ONE SPECIES OF FISH CALLED SARDINE

BY ROSALEEN LYNCH

FIRST PLACE WINNER

Mam wants a mermaid instead of me and though I slip
out of her like a fish in the birthing pool on a rainy day,
I have no tail or scales, and I do not smell of the sea,
and when Pa tries to give her this squalling too-many-
limbed me, she tells him 'Some cactuses don't grow
towards the light,' but she doesn't mind when I'm
swaddled and even though she's not got baby shoes or
any clothes with legs, she does not go out to buy them
and keeps me zipped up like a clam in sleeping-bag
suits or wraps me in layers of long seaweed coloured
shifts and smocks she ties with twine, and tells me
'Scales are like if cactus spines were flat, or umbrellas
closed when there's no rain,' and she does not encour-
age me to walk, so I sit with her as she tells me of her
dream of Pa and her dancing on the boardwalk at
Coney Island and she sings, 'Somewhere beyond the
sea…' or I lie on my back or belly to slide across the
floor, legs lost in the folds that follow, or I ride on Pa's
old skateboard with the scull and crossbones, a knot to
stop hems getting caught, and I sail out the back door

and down the garden path, like a minnow on a stream, and she calls me Guppy, Betta, or Angelfish and when she's angry Sprat, and when the time comes for me to start nursery she puts it off, saying she doesn't want to be left like a lone cactus on a dessert shore, me gone in the morning, Pa gone to security work at night and asleep in the day, until he comes to say goodbye to me out back, and stands in sunlight at the garden fence, hand over one eye to see, turning it into a telescope, to say 'I spy a mermaid swimming in the bluebell sea,' a bottle hanging from his other hand, uisce beatha, the water of life, company on the boat at night, that harbours the pirate radio-station, that Mam listens to, out of reach of the Gardaí, the guardians of the peace, and when Pa's gone Mam goes on the phone, request- ing songs, laughing like she's never done with Pa and waves from the bedroom window, the mermaid tail cactus he gave her on the sill and she looks past the field I'm in and down the hill to the sea, and the wind picks up, the net curtains fill like sail, and the air carries words of hers, like 'freedom', 'escape' and 'yes' and the wind vane turns and the white net curtain with it, to slap across Mam's body and shroud her face, a ghost now standing in the window, as if all that's left of her is the mermaid tail, and as I watch, I feel the bluebell sap stick my toes together, and I lie back in the grass and by my face in the bluebell sky hangs the first moon daisy which I pick and pluck the petals from to confirm I should spend that summer, weaving a mermaid's tail from dried seaweed, seagrass, long grass and weeds to hide in the shed, to show Mam when we come home, from her first day of work and mine of school, where I spend the hours kicking off my shoes, the teacher complaining about spills and falls and other children copying me, until the floor is littered with shoes and he tells me to pick up every one and return them, and I do, to the fish tank that has lost its fish and watch the shoes swim, laces flailing in the bubbles coming from the fake plastic treasure chest, and Mam has to come from the canning factory to pick me up, smelling of sardines and oil, and says, 'There are twenty-one species of fish called sardine,' and asks why can't I be one, as she lifts me up from the chair I was told to wait on, wrapping my duffle coat round my bare legs and feet, as she takes me to the car, and says, 'The sea urchin cactus only wakes at sunset,' and straps me in the front passenger seat and we drive, I can't see where, but it's not home, and the radio plays 'This is the sea' by the Water Boys and I fall asleep and wake in quiet until Mam's car door opens to let in the sound of the seagulls and sea and closes, and I slip out of the seat belt and up on my knees to lean on the warm dashboard, and watch through the windscreen, what she calls cactus clouds with little pricks of rain, roll in, as she disappears as if she was never there, into the sea, the rain making the glass between us a blur, and I switch on the radio, the orange light of the dial like a little sunset in the dark of the car and I remember the sea urchin cactus Mam said only woke at sunset as I listen to the presenter announce a special request, from The Last Pirate to his treasures at home and 'What shall we do with the drunken sailor' plays and dovetails into the traditional Irish song, 'Óró, sé do bheatha abhaile', O row, you are welcome home, making my neck prickle, and still leaning on the now cold dashboard, the skin on my arms goose-pimples and my legs go numb, as I wait for Mam to come out of the sea.

TWENTY-ONE SPECIES OF FISH CALLED SARDINE

FEARFUL SYMMETRY

BY HOLLY BARRATT

FIRST PLACE WINNER

I first met my sister when I was five. She was twice the size of a house cat, with a soft little bear-face, snowy whiskers and a baffled smile. She rolled over and stretched out her fluffy limbs. I instantly loved the pin cushion pads of her paws, and the wiggle of stripes as she shook herself out. She balance-walked up my body, rolled around on my belly, and then placed a paw on my nose. Her claws grazed my cheeks but I wasn't hurt. My sister wouldn't hurt me, ever. Her white throat moved up and down fast with either heartbeat or breathing, letting me know she was alive, alive.

'Hello,' I whispered, so as not to wake Mum and Dad. We shouldn't be playing at this time of night. My sister tilted her head then jumped onto the carpet, and batted at my red ball. I got out of bed, and rolled it across the room. She chased it, jumped on it, and attacked it with her teeth. It wrecked the ball but I didn't care. I didn't care at all. We played until the sun came up and she needed to go, because my sister is nocturnal.

She visited me most nights. We played ball. We curled up close in bed and I put my hand on her side to feel her rise and fall. She tried not to scratch or bite me, but sometimes she drew blood just because that's her nature. I never cried out or told her off because I knew she might never come back again.

Before I was born, my sister was like me. There are photographs of us both in frames on the wall by the stairs. Until I was four there were more of her than of me. Now there are more of me than there are of her. The living room has only one photograph, which sits on a corner shelf behind the arm of the sofa. You only see it if you decide to look at it. She is like me and not like me. She has dark yellow hair that drags across her forehead and into her ice-cream. Her eyes are screwed up because it's sunny and I can't see what colour they are. Mum says her eyes were brown like mine. Her teeth are blunt and wonky, with a gap near the front. Her skin is tan, and she wears a yellow hat. The picture reminds me of sand.

'The summer we lost her,' Mum told a visitor, before she went into the bathroom to be sick.

When I was seven, I noticed my sister getting bigger. She moved slow, like wading through water. Her pounces were exclamation marks at the end of a strolling sentence. She yawned often: showing the length of her fangs. She looked dangerous and I was glad she was my sister. I felt safe around her. If she could draw blood on me, imagine what she could do to an enemy.

'We don't keep photographs from that day,' Mum told another visitor. 'I deleted them all. I don't want to remember her that way.'

She had the picture in her lap.

'It helps to talk about her. To talk about her, not about what happened to her. There's no reason to relive that. I wouldn't want to upset Lily. She never knew her sister, but we always wanted her to see the happy, beautiful girl she always was.'

I spent nights with my sister, and by day I typed her name into the internet and read old newspaper articles. The articles asked questions: has the safari park improved safety? Is it right to keep beautiful wild animals in captivity? And there was a newer story, about someone else's sister, a zookeeper in another country.

My sister is full grown. She is bigger than me and can't lie on the bed without her back legs hanging off, so she lies mainly on the floor, licking her huge claws. I see blood on them, but it isn't mine, so I don't know what she eats before she visits. Although I told her to be quiet, sometimes she can't help but roar: she opens wide, her teeth like knives and the sound makes my bones vibrate. She makes the room stink of sugary pee, she leaves hairs on the carpet and she hurts me – she scraped a claw right down my left arm when I tried to hug her and it was so painful I thought I might faint. I wore long sleeves for weeks. The scar is ugly but I like to feel it and sometimes I want her to scar me more. My sister can't talk at all and all I want her to tell me is what it feels like to be ripped apart.

FEARFUL SYMMETRY BY HOLLY BARRATT © 2021.

HOLLY BARRATT GREW UP IN THE EAST MIDLANDS OF ENGLAND BUT NOW LIVES IN WALES. SHE HAS BEEN PUBLISHED BY LEAF BOOKS AND WAS LONGLISTED FOR THE 2019 BRICK LANE BOOKSHOP SHORT STORY COMPETITION. SHE IS CURRENTLY WORKING ON A NOVEL.

WHEN THE MONSTER IS HUNGRY

BY HOLLY KYBETT SMITH

COMPETITION FINALIST

Pay no mind to the tiger's pelt they shipped in from India, two years dead and still bright as a living flame. Heed not the electric telegraph; the express passenger locomotive they have called the *Lady of the Lake*. Walk through the art galleries without stopping to marvel; let the penny-guides flutter to the ground unread.

It's the mermaid you are here to see.

A decade has passed since the Great Exhibition of 1851. The Empire is hurting as it grows, just like you, with all the collateral pain of wisdom teeth and lengthening bones. It is hungry all the time, reaching out for new treasure and thoughts; sinking deft incisors into each nourishing morsel as your own sink into hot and greasy meat. You are afraid of yourself, living in your boarding house alone. Sometimes you lie awake, attuned to the breaths of girls in other rooms, and wonder whether you're becoming a monster. Sometimes you fear you might die before you find out.

Though the Empire might share your appetite, it

does not share your anxieties. The Empire is bigger than you, so much bigger, and stronger, and it is not constricted by the limits of a body: like a living ship of Theseus it redesigns itself, assimilating what it likes into its bulk, replacing the old with new. It's a bare-faced young immortal, audacious and lavish, and you think the empty tiger skin says it all – a summary in orange – which must be why they brought it here.

But it's the mermaid you are here to see.

They found her swimming off the east coast of Ceylon. Brought her back to England in a barrel, along with a shipment of coffee. (You have dreamed about that boat ride, though you have never yourself seen the ocean. Your dreams are of close and sloshing darkness; of nausea you can taste, all coffee beans and salt.) Since then, she has become the subject of every natural scientist's pamphlet and magazine: the type of lofty document you don't take yourself seriously enough to read, but wish very much that you did. They have classified her as a mammal, you have heard, for her hair and her breasts. They believe she can survive on land, but only in brief snatches. The dark air of London makes her cry. They feed her on raw fish and kelp and she devours both with sharp, sharp teeth.

She does not speak to the professors; not in English, French, Tamil or Sinhala.

You would like to see what her eyes say.

The Exhibition has not been open long, so the crowds of visitors have yet to lose their fervour. Outside, May sunshine drifts listless through the trails of factory smoke; breezes stir the plant-life in the gardens of the Royal Horticultural Society. You tread around litter, newspapers and grease-spotted food wrappings blowing down the paths. You would like to stop and eat – you forgot this morning – but you do not stop; do not dare to keep her waiting.

Inside, bodies press thickly together, heating up the air, which rises and condenses on the glass of the great ceiling domes at either entrance. A pianist performs beneath the Western dome, where you enter. A dainty noise drowned out by the clamour of excited voices.

You pass through the crowd with eyes cast upward, feeling – in the hazy light – as though you are trapped under a crinoline. As though the building they commissioned for this momentous event is a body itself; a living thing; a giantess. And you, perhaps a flea.

But it's the mermaid you are here to see.

There are so many different wings and alcoves in this place – so many ways you might get lost – but you keep your ears pricked, following the whispers of the crowd. The mermaid is the star of this exhibit, and they have her front-and-centre, her tank like a heart with its pumps and tubes and valves.

The first glimpse you catch is of her hair. Dark in the water, tendril-like, silky and loose. The sight sends an animal jolt through you, a desire that propels you one step closer, two. It does not matter how many bodies block your path. Your elbows clear the way, propriety forgotten. What is propriety when her body is calling out to yours? What is propriety when you are ravenous?

You shove and elbow and barge, your wide skirt doing some of the work but not all. Your corset is old and one of the stays jabs at your armpit, sharp and cruel. You do not care.

It's the mermaid you are here to see.

The mermaid who will answer your question: *am I really a monster?*

Did he who made the Lamb make me?

You have dreamed of this moment: the moment your tough and needle-deadened fingertips make contact with the glass. The moment you stare into her eyes.

For weeks now, you have been keeping yourself up at night, wondering what constitutes monstrosity. Is it as the Empire says – the tiger, with its teeth and claws designed to kill and eat, its body engineered to consume other bodies raw? Is it the mermaid, with her thick blubbery tail and her sweet humanlike face, her fingers webbed but still capable of holding a pen?

Is it you, is it you, is it you?

One look in her eyes is all you need. One look, to tell you whether there is kinship there; whether she and you are of a kind.

But the glass is dull when you reach it. The water, too, dull and brownish like it was drawn from the Thames. Bubbles cough through it, not the silvery things you had been picturing but clouded orbs that vanish into silt. And the mermaid's eyes may be open, but you know that she isn't looking back.

WHEN THE MONSTER IS HUNGRY BY HOLLY KYBETT SMITH © 2021.

HOLLY KYBETT SMITH IS A 22-YEAR-OLD LESBIAN, HISTORY LOVER AND WRITER OF GOTHIC FICTION. HAVING RECENTLY GRADUATED FROM THE UNIVERSITY OF WINCHESTER WITH A BA IN CREATIVE WRITING, SHE IS NOW HOPING TO EMBARK ON A CAREER THAT LETS HER STRING WORDS TOGETHER TO HER HEART'S CONTENT. HER NON-FICTION WORK HAS BEEN FEATURED ON TOR.COM

AND HER FICTION IN ISSUE #2 OF THE NEW GOTHIC REVIEW.

DOG ON BALCONY. NO DOG ON BALCONY

BY PHILIP CHARTER

COMPETITION FINALIST

My heart jumps into my throat and stays there. A slip, a scramble, two floors down, then *crack*, he hits the pavement with a yelp. The wind roars but the dog lies perfectly still — an off-white rug, tossed onto the street. Grab a jacket. Take the stairs two at a time. I push my way into the howl.

Our balconies line up perfectly, his across the street from mine. The dog has a big house, two girls that love him, and a marble patio table to shield the sun as he watches the street below. I live alone. My table has a cork mat under one leg. We have a connection, *Cappuccino* and me. He listens while I talk about Maria. We watch the weekend crowds pass with their bright blue coolboxes and beach towels.

My hand rests on his scruffy chest. 'Easy, boy.' Up and down, up and down. Blood leaks from one ear. Rain and street water slick his fur. He'll be cold. The impact punched his jaw to an ugly angle. Action. I get up and hammer on their door. No answer. The wind whips away my shouts and carries them out to sea. Two blocks to the vet. I roll him into the jacket and hoist him into my arms. He weighs more than the weekly box of vegetables Juanjo delivers, slightly less than my Maria at the end. 'Easy, boy.'

The dog was there when we moved in. They left him outside as a puppy, even though he was small enough to fit through the bars. Maria named him *Cappuccino* because of his brown-white swirls. We never asked his real name. She threw him scraps of *chorizo* while we sipped coffee. When we finished she would tip the grounds onto a saucer and look for clues. 'Oh, you have a big surprise coming,' she'd say. Then she would kiss me with her caffeine-stained lips.

My arms burn and the salt rain stings my eyes. I make it to the vet, panting. The dog whimpers under the jacket. The puny electronic bell sounds. Nothing. I press it again. Finally, a wild-eyed man in a white coat opens the door. 'What a gale! . . . from the balcony? . . . how nasty.'

The waiting room offers little to read. Screens replay scenes with happy dogs running through grassy fields. As I wait, my mind casts back to the hours spent holding Maria's hand in the chemotherapy ward. She didn't see that one in the coffee grounds.

The white-coat returns and says they'll keep *Cappuccino* overnight. Nothing more for me to do. I nod gravely and go home to sit in my own waiting room. Outside my building, I discover my cup has blown off the balcony and smashed on the ground, its black grit seeping. By evening, the winds have died. Shutters roll up, cafes turn their signs to *open* and neighbours venture out onto their balconies to smoke and consider the brooding sky.

Later, my neighbour comes to offer his thanks. He thrusts a bottle of brandy at me. 'Please, enjoy this. I'm not going to drink it, and it's a good one.' I wasn't even sure of *his* name. 'And here's your jacket back.'

'I don't drink brandy,' I say. 'I drink coffee.' What a ridiculous thing to say.

He takes a step back and lifts his gaze from the bottle to my weathered face.

'Thanks anyways . . .' I take the bottle and wrap it tight in the jacket. 'What's his name, the dog?'

'Angel.' The man shrugs. 'My girls named him.' Strange. He's not a graceful dog. 'Angel' rests his arthritic bones most of the day and barks like he smokes forty a day.

My neighbours keep him inside now, occasionally dragging him to the beach for some air. I drink coffee facing an empty balcony across the street. They put a tall plant out there, but it doesn't survive the winds. The brandy lives in the cabinet, next to the good china. Every time I take a cup from the shelf, the glaring space left by the broken one seems bigger, more painful. Nothing but a ring of dust. Sometimes, I dream of hurling the other cups down to smash on the street, creating more space in the cabinet. Instead, I sit and wait for the next storm to come.

DOG ON THE BALCONY. NO DOG ON THE BALCONY
BY PHILIP CHARTER © 2021.

PHILIP CHARTER IS A BRITISH WRITER WHO TEACHES
WRITING TO NON-NATIVE ENGLISH SPEAKERS. HIS WORK
HAS BEEN FEATURED IN FLASHBACK FICTION AND THE
NATIONAL FLASH FICTION DAY ANTHOLOGY. IN 2018, HE

RELEASED HIS DEBUT SHORT FICTION COLLECTION, FOREIGN
VOICES. HE LIKES ORANGE CATS, BUT HATES ORANGES.

BARKING MAD

BY RICHARD FROST

COMPETITION FINALIST

The dog wandered in uninvited. No collar. No tag. A mongrel with a few identifiable features. And others less certain in origin.

I've had unwelcome guests before. But the arrival of 'The Dog', as I decided to call the canine visitor, was, initially, quite comforting. Someone to talk to. Someone who would listen. Someone who would help me feel sorry for myself. A stray looking for a home, so I gave it one. Won't be here long, I thought. It'll soon go off and find someone else to be with.

Well, I was wrong there, that's for sure. The longer The Dog stayed, the harder it became. A voracious appetite eating me out of home, not house. I fed it too much as well. Following me everywhere. Incessantly barking. Filling my mind like a discordant earworm. I thought distraction would be the better part of valour. And at times it was. But I've been an avoider all my life.

I was pulled to unfamiliar places. Sometimes slowly. Other times fast. Picking up mess as we went along. Occasionally a disconcerting mix of all four. Not nice.

Night was the worst. Repeatedly licking my head. Sleep broken by kicks to the stomach. Waking to find myself well and truly sat on.

A highly-strung pedigree also made its presence felt.

That one got its teeth into me on more than one occasion. It still hangs around a bit even now.

It got so bad I started snapping.

I should have asked for help sooner. Even if I had, I probably wouldn't have actually done anything.

I knew what others would say. At least I thought I did. 'It needs to know who's boss.' 'Why did you let it get this bad?' 'Stop feeling sorry for yourself.' A few spoken. Most not. But the thoughts had already counted.

'It's me or The Dog.'

That was scary. I wanted to let go of the lead.

'We could try some medication,' said the expert. 'And maybe some CBT.'

'What, Canine Behavioural Therapy?' I said. It was the first joke I'd made in ages. At least they smiled. I wasn't totally mad, then.

It's taken effort I didn't want to make, to be honest. A long time too – lot longer than expected. I guess if I'd… oh well, we can all look back on our mistakes, even if they weren't at the time. I could have done things differently. But I didn't.

But I am now. Now I'm the one controlling the lead.

Occasionally, I'll get sat on for a bit. Sometimes, I let it run free – but not for too long. Most of the time, I'm the only one in bed too: can't tell you what a relief that was.

In fact, we're pretty good friends. I know the dog and the dog knows me. I might even give it a name. Or would they think I'm mad?

BARKING MAD BY RICHARD FROST © 2021.

61

UNTIL RETIRING FROM PAID EMPLOYMENT THREE YEARS AGO, RICHARD FROST HAS BEEN HELPING PEOPLE FOR WHOM A HEALTH PROBLEM AFFECTED THEIR ABILITY TO FIND OR REMAIN IN EMPLOYMENT. HE SPECIALIZED IN HELPING THOSE EXPERIENCING MENTAL ILL HEALTH AND WAS APPOINTED AN MBE FOR THAT WORK. HE IS ALSO A LAY MINISTER IN THE CHURCH OF ENGLAND AND PUB-LISHED WRITER (BOOKS, ARTICLES, BOOK REVIEWS - NON-FICTION).

OUR TRANSFORMATIONS

BY DAVID HARTLEY

Ancient

Your Cthulhu was being put to sleep. He was slumped against your legs, tentacles withered.

'He's outdated,' you said, scratching behind a drooped wing, 'hasn't moved with the times.' The ancient one attempted a shrug, but even that was too much effort.

A vet nurse advised us to hold our creatures close while Cthulhu's life-force was ended. I cradled Scorchio, my phoenix, let him lick the flame of my lighter. The air thinned, colours span, terror streaked through our minds.

As soon as you emerged, the maelstrom stopped. You were distraught, you were beautiful, and I offered you my seat.

Hydran

There was a sense, I think, that it was far too early for me to meet your mother. But in the rush of our passion, we'd abandoned calendars and her beheading was days overdue. Would I be a love and lend a hand?

She was spitty and snappy and kept accusing me of taking advantage of a vulnerable woman. I protested but you shushed me, told me to grip her hair and hold her steady. Your axe cut was clean. We passed a passionless night as the new head grew in. This one liked me better.

Jackalope

When Scorchio had exhausted his rebirths, we scattered his ashes on Mam Tor and watched the sunrise. It was our most perfect day. We should have let that settle, but in a haste to cheer me up, you rushed out the next day and got us a jackalope; a rabbit with antlers.

It hated me. It took every chance it could to rut my legs and make me bleed. We had the antlers sawn to stubs, and it soon became my job to keep them filed down. Quietly, gently, slowly, we bonded, and now we're inseparable. But the scars at my ankles often itch.

Labyrinthine

The rule in our house had always been: the less said about my brother, the better. But Christmas takes you over and fills you through, and I'd guilted you into spending it with my family, and you were missing yours. So, you stole out with a plateful of meat, unlocked the labyrinth, and followed the thread to the centre.

I do not know what passed in those stone walls that night, but I often wonder. When you returned you were giddy and bruised. When we asked you how he was, all you could say was: 'He's fine. He's totally fine.'

Medusan

Your punishment was to weave snakes into your hair and stare at me until I turned to stone. I passed a year in that pathetic pose, the words *she meant nothing to me* carved across my thigh. I could make no protest as you wrestled me into the front garden and had me hoisted onto a plinth. People came to see. They spat and smirked at my privy member, just as forlorn as the rest.

My time served, and the snakes dead, you called in the Aphoditans to kiss me back to life. I had to apologise for that too.

Equine

When our son was born a centaur, we argued about who had the equine DNA. I cited your love of frolicking wild through meadows, your mane-like hair, your stubbornness. As if to prove my latter point, you fixated on my apple habit, and the three lumps of sugar I always have in my tea. There was no getting around it, so it simmered. Only when Billy got old enough to learn biology did he suggest it was probably a little from column A, a little from column B. That earned him an expensive pair of Adidas horseshoes, our bright lad.

Maiden

I know of a method, you said, to turn mermaid, you said, a place in the woods, a copper bath, in the midday sun of All Saints Day, you said, and you invoked the *I'd do anything for you, babe*, promise; something I'd said, at our wedding vows.

So, we had a sober Halloween, drove through dawn, and set everything up in Wych Elm Wood in the Malverns. This is it, you said, heat up the water, you said, I love you, you said, as you wriggled your toes in the mulch of leaves and muttered your goodbyes to them.

Siren

You slicked and slipped through oil barons, carved their eco lies across their chests; you rode cascades to douse forest fires, burning brands on the asses of naysayers; you moulded a throne from polymers on the Pacific trash vortex and lured world leaders to be wrecked at your feet.

When they interviewed me, I fluffed my lines. The best word I could summon was *inspiration*, which fell so flat. You called and said the footage made your heart leap, said you thought of me and Billy every day. I felt lured, but I plugged my ears. You never came home.

Saint

The last great act of the Catholic Church was to canonise you, the saviour of the world. The doorway to the Hall of Saints flung open. The flayed Bartholomew met you at the threshold, his skin draped over his arm. He asked you something and you turned to point at me. I waved.

You stepped inside and transformed. You became as you were martyred: a snow flurry, tears of icicles. I cried too, but nothing I had done would get me through that door. So, I stayed with your mother, and all her heads, taking the rough with the smooth.

OUR TRANSFORMATIONS BY DAVID HARTLEY © 2021.

DAVID HARTLEY WRITES STRANGE STORIES ABOUT STRANGE THINGS FOR STRANGE PEOPLE. HE HOLDS A PHD IN CREATIVE WRITING FROM THE UNIVERSITY OF MANCHESTER AND IS CURRENTLY TRYING TO FLOG AN EXPERIMENTAL NOVEL ABOUT AUTISTIC GHOSTS. HE IS THE AUTHOR OF THE SHORT STORY COLLECTIONS INCORCISMS (ARACHNE PRESS) AND FAUNA (FLY ON THE WALL PRESS), BOTH RELEASED IN 2021. HE LIVES IN MANCHESTER.

SCHRÖDINGER'S DOVES

BY L F MILLS

'The doves are dead.' Bernie said, his voice low.

'You're not serious? How?'

'I left them in the car during the ceremony. They must have overheated.' Bernie indicated the bow-topped box on the floor at his feet.

Earlier that day, when the handler had given him the box, Bernie had heard a gentle rustling of feathers and the occasional coo. Now the box was silent, its finely decorated exterior at odds with the potential disaster that lay within.

Because it was a disaster. Bernie was best man. Reg was counting on him to release a flock of white doves as he and his bride left the church. Which was due to happen any second. He couldn't let Reg down again, not after the catastrophe of the stag night.

'What's going on?' Ben asked sidling over from a gaggle of bridesmaids.

Just what I need, Bernie thought, another grooms-man getting involved.

'Bernie's killed the doves!' said John.

'You're kidding? How?' Ben asked, amusement

creeping into his voice.

'It doesn't matter!' Bernie said, before John could answer. 'What am I going to do?'

'Well. Are you sure they're dead? I mean, have you looked in the box?' Ben asked. He picked the box up from the floor. It was heavy, a carved wooden crate, with a polished brass latch to keep the birds contained. Ben shifted the box from side to side, trying to feel if there was life inside, but the wood was heavy and any evidence of activity was obscured.

'Should we open it?' John suggested.

Bernie shook his head dully and replied, 'I already thought of that, but what if they're not dead and they all fly out? Reg will kill me.'

'Schrödinger's doves.' Ben muttered, with one ear to the box.

'What?'

'We don't know if they're dead or alive. The only way to find out is to open the box.' He explained, 'And we can't do that until the happy couple leave the church. Of course, doves and pigeons are, scientifically speaking, exactly the same. There's no real distinction between them other than colouring.'

As he spoke, Ben's eyes followed a couple of bedraggled wood pigeons pecking aimlessly by the wheels of the wedding cars.

Bernie put his hand to his head.

'We're *not* releasing pigeons.' He said through gritted teeth.

'Fine, then release the doves and see what happens.' Ben handed the box back to Bernie and sauntered back to his position by the bridesmaids, undoubtedly planning to share a joke at Bernie's predicament.

'What are you going to do?' asked John, as Bernie shook the box fruitlessly, praying for a sign.

'I'll have to open it and see won't I? I'll have to tell Reg I messed up again.' Bernie's tone was steady, but his eyes were heartbroken

'It'll be ok.' John patted him awkwardly on the arm, 'Let's take a peek now. If we're quick we can shut it before they all get out.'

As he spoke, a harried looking photographer swept out of the church doors and began ushering the guests into position. He pointed at Bernie and John, forcing them to take their positions on the lowest step of the church.

The bride and groom appeared, to a chorus of cheers and a shower of confetti. Bernie took a deep breath as the photographer pointed his lens towards him. Reg caught his eye and gave him a cheery wink.

Bernie opened the box.

SCHRÖDINGER'S DOVES BY L F MILLS © 2021.

L F MILLS IS AN AUTISTIC, FEMALE, HORROR WRITER, WITH A SPECIAL INTEREST IN PSYCHOLOGICAL HORROR AND A GUILTY PLEASURE FOR ZOMBIES. CURRENTLY, SHE IS WORKING ON HER SECOND NOVEL, A FEMINIST POST-APOCALYPTIC SURVIVAL STORY. SHE ALSO WORKS AS A MARKETING CONSULTANT ON FINANCIAL LITERATURE, WHICH DOESN'T LEAVE A LOT OF ROOM FOR HORROR, BUT PAYS THE BILLS.

THE WOLF AND THE DEER

BY LUCAS CAMMACK

'Venn-ison diagram.'

The doe stepped out from the undergrowth into a small, moonlit clearing in the woods, casting her shadow across the grass at the edge of the clearing. The wolf, who had been following the scent of the deer, saw the shadow and its owner immediately. The wolf crouched, hidden in the darkness of the brush opposite the clearing from the deer. As the wolf inched closer to the clearing, a night bird, perched in the nearby bushes, called out and took flight. With the commotion, the deer instinctively sprang back from the clearing and into the woods. The wolf ran forward, but by the time it had crossed the open patch the deer was gone, hurtling through the forest. The wolf, having gone days without a meal larger than a mouse, leaned into the pursuit and dove into the trees.

◆ ◆ ◆

Simpson woke early.

It would still be hours before the sun silvered the horizon, but there was much to be done. His crew had been behind for weeks, and the pressure to complete the job was mounting. He slowly pressed himself up on tired arms and slid out of bed as so not to disturb his wife.

Carrah had slept horribly most nights since the kids had gone. Her ears were always awake it seemed, listening for the children, wanting to be needed. He knew better than to make a sound, even credibly, while she could have some semblance of rest. He stood with a creak in his old bones, and looked at her still sleeping, and then slipped out of the bedroom.

The night before he had made his lunch and his coffee in leu of the early day and had deposited them in the passenger seat of his old ford. The coffee in the thermos would be stale and barely warm, the sandwiches soggy and near frozen, but shoddy provisions were preferrable to an even more tired version of his already haggard wife.

He moved in his socks and briefs silently to the living room, where his work clothes sat in a rumpled, dark mass in the corner. He whispered his way into his pants and shirt, but opted to don his coat and boots out on the front porch. The heavy material of the coat and his footsteps in his boots would have been a veritable cacophony in the pre-dawn still.

Simpson stepped outside the front door and eased it shut with a click and slid into his old boots and wrestled on his coat in the parched, cold air.

He walked softly across the gravel, and out to his truck at the end of the drive, parked away from the house to buffer the sound of his departure. He opened the truck door and slid in behind the wheel and put the keys in the ignition and turned over the engine as he closed the door, consolidating his sounds, even fifteen yards away from the house. As the motor sputtered to life, KCXI's morning selection of Golden Oldies came blaring from the truck's tinny speakers. He cursed under his breath; he had forgotten to turn off the radio when he had arrived home the night before. He quickly twisted the volume nob down, silencing the music.

He sat and listened to the engine gurgle beneath the hood, and he watched the house. No light from the bedroom, no sound of her calling for him or the kids.

He waited, still nothing, save for the motor and his heart beating and his breath misting in the cold air of the truck cab under the crystal moonlight and stars.

All clear, he idled out of the driveway and onto the frozen, dark, chip-sealed road.

◆ ◆ ◆

The deer flashed through occasional patches of moonlight in between the trees as the wolf gained on the form that carved the way for them both through the dense brush. The deer felt the wolf closing in, but just as the carnivore was upon her, she turned sharply and sprinted up a rise towards the small road that ran through the woods. The wolf lost ground but followed on.

The road was mostly unused, but this night the wolf heard the hiss of tires approaching where the deer, and, soon after, the wolf, would cross. The deer heard the approaching car too, but her fear pressed her forward, as did hunger prod the wolf.

Hooves clomped, feet scurried, tires sizzled. The

lights of the vehicle peered through the grass and tall weeds at the roadside, silhouetting the deer as it leapt into the road.

◆ ◆ ◆

Carrah woke with a start. She had heard something loud, a crash, like something falling perhaps. She sat still and tried to place the noise. She breathed and listened, but heard nothing, and then thought maybe it was just the sounds of her dreams waking her again, dreams of the children playing in the house, in the kitchen, jamming on pots and pans or rolling toys down the basement stairs. She lay back again and reached across the bed to her husband, but there was nothing on his side of the bed save for the shallow depression where he had laid through the night. The spot was still warm, and she wondered for a moment where he was, but then remembered: early shift, overtime, the big project. She lay still and listened for longer.

The night was silent and dark, the children were gone, her husband was too. She was alone, and so she rolled over and fell back into her dreams of happier days, days of laughter, when the home was full and warm, and the lights beamed out the windows and into the darkness amongst the trees.

THE WOLF AND DEER BY LUCAS CAMMACK © 2021.

LUCAS CAMMACK IS AN AMERICAN EXPAT LIVING IN NEW ZEALAND. HE IS A BUILDER AND FATHER THESE DAYS, BUT HAS LIVED A FEW LIVES. IN THE 90'S, HE WAS A DRUNKEN POET, ARTIST AND COUNTRY MUSO. IN THE 2000'S, HE WAS A YOGA TEACHER WITH

GLOBAL ACCLAIM. HIS PAINTS AND GUITARS ARE STILL CLOSE AT HAND. BUT HE FINDS WITH THE PARTNER AND BUBS AND TIME THAT MESS AND NOISE AREN'T ALWAYS THE BEST THING.

THE HORNBEAM'S LAMENT

BY HELEN WILLIAMS

NEW VOICE AWARD WINNER

Autumn 1901

The axes, saws and chains came that autumn. I was only 82 years old then. They cleared the land to build the house, removing the woodland around me with indecent haste. The sounds of the crashing branches as they felled my family haunt me still. Then, they stopped, and left me, a lone specimen marking the boundary between the lawned garden and the landscape beyond.

I miss my siblings. I miss the competition to see who could grow tall enough to touch the sky and the feel of our roots mingling in the Kentish sandy soil. I learned to listen to the song of the trees from far away across the downs; the low undertones of the oaks and the sweet murmurings of the willows.

Summer 1902

First I heard chatter and laughter from the house, then it came from the terrace getting closer each day. Suddenly he was by my side, tilting his curious face up towards my crown. 'I am six' he announced, 'how old are you?' Unexpectedly he wrapped his arms as far as they would reach around my trunk, pressing himself close against my mottled trunk. Taking care to mark the furthest spot with his fingertips he circled around me, repeating this manoeuvre three more times to measure my full circumference. Then he ran off, zig-zagging across the lawn.

No human had ever touched me before. I was accustomed to the squirrels scittering along my branches and the fluttering finches stealing my papery seeds, but this was exquisitely different. Over the next few days the boy returned, exploring my pleated leaves and delicately investigating my twisted bark.

'Stanley Michael Edward Dunmore! You come back here this very instant!' the female in a long black skirt and lacey shirt shouted from the terrace. That was the first time he climbed up along my branches, pressing his back securely against my trunk. He stifled his giggling laugh so as not to give his location away. They could not find him, it was as if he had just disappeared.

Summer 1911

He was lying in a deckchair on the lawn, his arms folded, with a book shading his eyes from the ardent sun. He had grown into a tall, thin sapling, his hair now darkened to sandy brown. In the stillness of summer we both dozed and breathed deeply the shimmering air.

Winter 1914

I had seen many winters but few felt as bleak as this, after days of ceaseless rain, the temperature dropped, bringing fitful snow flurries. He stood at the window, watching, waiting. We heard the men marching up the lane on their way to the docks. We felt their boots stomping the ground like a pulse ebbing away.

Summer 1915

We were so proud of him dressed in his uniform. His sister took photographs on the lawn. He stood tall and let my shadow rest gentle across his shoulder.

Spring 1916

On those few precious days when he was home on leave, he would go out early and walk for hours; trying to muster peaceful sleep through exhaustion. I wanted to cradle him on my beams and hide him, but most days he would just pass me by. Finally, on that last morning, he climbed up into my branches once more. His khaki green drab amongst my fresh furled leaves. I knew he would look for my fellow hornbeams in France and that their familiar shape would give him comfort and protection if they could. He pulled a button from his tunic and placed it in the crook one of my branches.

Summer 1916

The sounds of the guns grew louder from across the water and the murmurs of the petrified trees retreated as they were shattered and scattered by the artillery.

After the telegram boy cycled away, I could hear the heartbreak spilling through the open terrace doors. It flowed across the lawn and down into my roots. I lashed my branches, whipping them around, flinging my accusations through the air towards the hornbeams of Delville Wood. The sighs came back on the wind like sobbing waves, 'We fell, they fell. We fell, they fell.'

They could not find him. It was as if he had just disappeared.

Spring 1962

She was a curious looking creature in flared trousers and a knitted waistcoat. She ran through the low gate at the edge of the lawn, letting it slap shut behind her. She hardly paused before reaching up to my lower branches, wedging her plimsoled feet against my trunk and pulling herself up. When she planted her small hands on my rough bark, I knew she would be the one. She settled high enough to be hidden from view under my crisp canopy.

I could hear her Grandmother calling to her from the terrace. The girl found the button as she was climbing down. 'Look Granny. Look what I found.' The old woman peered at the blackened disc in the child's hand. She recognised the insignia.

'That belonged to my brother. The soldier in the photographs. He was lost, at Delville Wood, on the Somme. '

Summer 1984

When she grew up, the little girl kept the promise I heard her make to her Granny that day; to find the boy who had first climbed the tree and mark his resting place. I knew that the naked trees had fallen in on him, as I had begged them to, protecting his lifeless body from further desecration by the relentless shells, but I never dreamed that it would take so long for them to find him.

She told me the military had replanted Delville

Wood, as a sacred monument, but, she confided, not with hornbeams.

Spring 2019

My roots mingle with the new trees that have grown up all around me. I am 200 years old now. I will not grow much taller, but at noon my shadow rests on the empty terrace and my branches can almost touch the sky.

THE HORNBEAM'S LAMENT BY HELEN WILLIAMS © 2021.

HELEN WILLIAMS IS A FORMER ACCOUNTANT, WHO IS SLOWLY REPLACING HER APPRECIATION OF NUMBERS WITH A LOVE FOR WORDS. SHE WAS BORN IN WALES BUT HAS SPENT MOST OF HER LIFE LIVING OUTSIDE OF THE PRINCIPALITY, WHICH EXPLAINS HER INHERITED LOVE OF RUGBY AND SINGING LOUDLY.

THE MYCOLOGIST

BY LOUIS ROSSI

COMPETITION FINALIST

She washes her hair and tries not to look at it. It wasn't there yesterday.

A mushroom grows in the corner of her shower, sprouting from the crack between the filthy tiles. It glistens with moisture, flesh-like, rubicund.

She thinks *'I need a new apartment.'* She thinks *'I need a new job.'*

◆ ◆ ◆

Later. She works at her desk and doesn't think of the mushroom. She thinks only of the mushroom. She pushes her mouse around, pecks at the keyboard, sends an email. Thinks *'I should probably call the landlord.'* Then *'I can't wait that long.'*

At the store. She selects a bottle of fungicide, reads the label, puts it back. Selects another. This one. She pays for her purchase and leaves.

◆ ◆ ◆

The bathroom door stands ajar. She finds her eyes are drawn to it. She watches TV. She watches the door. The light bleeds from the day and the bathroom is lost in shadow. She can no longer see it from where she's sat. The thought is unbearable to her.

She gets up. Retrieves her purchases. Walks determinedly for the bathroom and draws back the shower curtain.

It's bigger already, and in the gloom of the shower stall seems almost to glow with some sickly inner light. She feels as if it knows she's there. That's insanity.

She takes up the bottle, depresses the trigger. Droplets bead on its dark, membranous gills. The bottle in her hand reads *Rapid-Gro.* She can no longer read it.

She returns for the second item, the one she doesn't remember buying. She tears the bag open with her fingernails and scoops up the dark, loamy soil with her bare hands. She turns the shower on low.

She sits monk-like in the tub as steam enshrouds them both.

LOUIS ROSSI IS A PROFESSIONAL WRITER AND ADVERTISING CREATIVE ORIGINALLY HAILING FROM DORSET, ENGLAND. IN 2018 HE EMIGRATED TO VANCOUVER CANADA, WHERE HE DRAWS INSPIRATION FROM THE STUNNING NATURAL LANDSCAPES AND DIVERSE WILDLIFE OF THE PACIFIC NORTHWEST.

CORVID EPIDEMIC CURE

BY SHARON BOYLE

That summer we were plagued by crows. From my hunched position on the stairs I heard Gran say, 'Jess and me'll make a scarecrow.'

'With a machine gun,' Grandpa grunted. 'Those crows are not feart of anything.' He broke off to yell up for Dad to get out his lazy pit.

Grandpa was a bellower of great fortitude. I could hear his gripes no matter where on the farm he was. Perhaps if we stuck Grandpa in the ground, the crow problem might be sorted.

After he left, I made for the barn, a shrine to all things broken, warped and ineffectual. I collected enough bits and pieces for scarecrow-making and returned to the house to find Gran rattling through her sewing box. She held up two tartan buttons.

'We'll use these for the eyes.'

I wrapped a burst football in a tea-towel and sewed on the buttons. Black wool became a stringy coiffure and a red, round ball chewed by Laddie the dog, long gone, made the nose. Gran stuffed potato bags with straw and dressed them in a pair of Grandpa's ripped trousers and a plaid shirt with armpits stiff with old sweat.

Gran stepped back from our creation. 'Jesus, it's the

spit of your Dad. Especially the nose.' Being of a holy bent she added, 'God forgive me.'

We carried our creation to the nearest field and staked it in.

'Flap freely!' I cried into the wind, which had roused itself for the occasion.

The scarecrow fluttered and whipped as if we had given it life. I danced around it, arms high, whooping until Gran stated that a thirteen-year-old lass shouldn't be cavorting like a carthorse.

'That's a fine looking tattiebogle youse have got there,' said Dad, cruising up behind us, a top note of whisky on his breath. 'Almost handsome, I'd say.'

'Aye, it was a morning's work.' Gran kept her eyes on the scarecrow.

'We're calling him Bolan,' I said, 'after Gran thinking he has mad hair like that T-Rex bloke.'

Dad grinned. 'Marc Bolan? Now there's a twentieth-century fella who can get it on.'

'I wish you'd get it on finding a job.' Gran craned round to look at him.

'I cannae find a job,' flared Dad, humour snuffed. 'Not with my back.'

'How's Margery?' Granny was not a woman who bothered with delicacies, owing to her brass-necked belief that all religious folk had God at their back giving them a celestial thumbs-up.

My eyes flicked to the house – to the window with the drawn curtains. Mum would be lying in bed, no doubt staring at the ceiling, her fingers gripping the top of the covers.

Dad slit his eyes, grumbled something about folk minding their own business and staggered off, ready to skive, complain and be a nuisance under Grandpa's feet.

Gran stared after him. 'Dinnae be looking in your Da's direction for an example of a good man, Jess. Look in your Grandpa's.'

I said nothing for it seemed to me that good men like Grandpa were allergic to fun. And I didn't fancy marrying anyone if the alternative was a drinking, swearing, laugh-at-anything man like Dad, who woke me up a week later doing all three. I opened my window and saw him in the night gloom, chatting to Bolan.

'Hey, dollybirdie,' he lisped. 'Don't be shy.'

Bolan's aloofness did not deter him. He placed a bold arm round the scarecrow's waist, yelping as the structure collapsed.

I was the one who had to repair Bolan. I re-stuffed and re-crucified him, cursing out my lungs in a way that made the crows think the next generation of fierce shouters was on its way. My throat nipped for I'd already spent a good hour standing at the bottom of Mum's bed, demanding she get hold of her senses; to stop drinking gin and tanking pills; that Dad romancing loose women was one thing but scarecrows quite another. I rummaged in her wardrobe for clothes for Bolan, creating enough clatter that she finally hefted back the covers.

'Here's a suitable dress,' she rasped, plucking one out.

◆ ◆ ◆

The following week Dad put on his best suit, filled a suitcase and slipped out the house. I'd been standing at the landing window watching Bolan and so witnessed him going.

A creak on the floorboards behind me – Mum, wan-faced and shivery.

'Gran and I are gutting the barn later,' I told her.

'Today must be the day for junk purging,' she whispered, placing a hand on my shoulder as if to steady herself. She had yelled at Dad last night until he squawked he was leaving.

We watched Dad slow his step to glance back.

Perhaps it was the scarecrow's dress that caught his eye – the white lace flitting and snapping, the veil swooping and soaring. The scarecrow looked fearsome, right enough, like a demented bride ready to uproot itself and hare after unwanted suitors.

Dad tugged his lapels together, cocked his head cityward and flapped out of sight.

CORVID EPIDEMIC CURE BY SHARON BOYLE © 2021.

SHARON BOYLE LIVES IN EAST LOTHIAN AND WRITES AROUND HER FAMILY AND PART-TIME JOB. SHE HAS HAD SEVERAL SHORT STORIES AND FLASH PIECES PUBLISHED ON-LINE AND IN MAGAZINES, INCLUDING HISSAC, EXETER WRITERS, WRITERS' FORUM AND CRANKED ANVIL. SHE TWEETS AS @SHARONBOYLE50

THE MUD

BY MICHELLE DONKIN ALLEN

Ruth didn't want to become one of those allotment people with their khaki trousers, fleece jackets and sensible shoes. She used to go to raves for goodness sake. She had one-night stands with men she met on dating apps. There was one man who walked with a limp and claimed to have no sense of smell after being hit on the nose with a cricket ball as a child.

She didn't want to be wandering around a garden centre on a Saturday afternoon, facing down an expensive ceramic planter in the shape of an owl and considering if it might liven up her life. And yet, here she was.

It had been a whim three years ago, after suddenly realising that Monty Don might actually be hot, that she listed her name on the council's waiting list. Now she had her very own allotment plot. Number 108, all 90 feet of overgrown weedy ground, was all hers for just £80 rent per year.

Ruth had never had outside space before. She had gone from her family's flat to her own and the entire concept of land being hers was mind-boggling. The sheer range of tools in the garden centre was all a little bit much.

Ignoring the pleading eyes of the ceramic owl, Ruth bought a few cheap tools: a spade, a fork, a trowel, and some gardening gloves. She walked them the three miles back through town to the allotment site, wondering if she would ever have the funds for a car, or if forty-three was too late to learn to drive.

Back at plot 108, Ruth sat down on a rock, her tools around her feet, blinking at the patch of land. Quite without warning, the darkness furled at the edges of her comprehension, threatening to crawl onwards as her stomach dropped in fear. A thought occurred to her in stark clarity: what if the darkness was not squashed by nature?

It was true that often, in her bleakest nights, she would lie on the bathroom floor and think about trees and plants. They existed in her mind as hopeful and eternal. Now she worried that coming here might destroy everything. She worried that some sadness about plants and nature would leave her with nothing to cling to on those nights that threatened to sink her. Never meet your heroes, they say.

Enough, Ruth told herself. She had the allotment now, she was going to use it. Grabbing her new cheap spade she pulled herself up from the rock and marched towards a particularly weedy looking area of ground, thrusting the blade into the mud.

Change happens slowly sometimes. It gently alters each part of a thing until that thing is different and no one can remember how it happened exactly. That day, in the allotment, change happened to Ruth in an instant.

If Ruth had been an animation film, her spade hitting the ground would have sent a bolt of light from the fissure in the earth and gold sparks would have reflected in Ruth's eyes. Her mouth would gape in anime awe and a sound of shocked delight would blast from her frozen face as the background whooshed by with white streaks of movement.

In reality, Ruth's body felt energised at each strike of spade with soil and each revelation of new mud under the tangle of knotted weeds.

Somehow, the act of digging seemed to chip away at Ruth's understanding of herself. Her calcified outer shell fell away. Beneath it, clear and real, ancient and instinctive, Ruth found a new shape. She was a farmer. She was descended from thousands of years of human existence. She was of the land. She belonged.

Lost in her task, Ruth moved down to her knees. She pulled out long thick roots with her gloved hands, even those that seemed to go on for miles beneath the ground. Mud stuck to her clothes, a thick dark cake mix, with fruits and nuts of stone.

Realisation came to her, fuzzy at first, then with clarity and calm. This mud was plant too, decomposed and now nurturing others in its turn. The greenest of new beginnings came from the very darkness of destruction itself.

Later, sitting back on her rock, Ruth surveyed the scene with new eyes. It was going to take a lot of work. The area she had cleared wasn't close to a quarter of the whole. Purpose sizzled at her, filling her with a sensation that took her a while to recognise.

Hope.

This patch of England needed her. She was obligated to it now that she had pushed down its natural will. She had a responsibility to manage and farm this place. She was needed.

Removing her gardening gloves, she found that the soil had crusted her fingers, having worked its way past the glove cuffs and down to her palms. It had pressed itself under her nails, fixing with her firmly. She was part mud now; part death and part nurture.

Perhaps, she decided, she was one of those allotment people after all, with their khakis trousers, fleece jackets and sensible shoes. They seemed more like curators of land now; trustees and keepers of a precious treasure: the mud and life itself.

THE MUD BY MICHELLE DONKIN ALLEN © 2021.

MICHELLE IS A WRITER AND COACH. SHE STUDIED SCREENWRITING AT NFTS AND WRITES FOR THE STAGE, SCREEN AND PAGE. IN 2021 SHE WAS SELECTED FOR THE CURTIS BROWN CREATIVE BREAKTHROUGH NOVEL WRITING SCHEME. MICHELLE IS THE CO-FOUNDER OF THEATRE COMPANY CAST IRON AND THE COMMUNITY ORGANISATION IRONCLAD CREATIVE, WHICH PROVIDES CAREER SUPPORT LOW-INCOME WRITERS AND THEATRE-MAKERS. SHE COACHES WRITERS AND CREATIVES THROUGH WWW.WRITEWITHMICHELLE.COM

THE OCEAN HE POURED INSIDE

BY PATRICK CLARKE

When I was barely a teenager, a friend pressed a conch shell to my flaky, sunburnt ear. We were sat a few feet back from the ocean's edge, as I never liked open water — it always made me feel like plants were slowly bursting out of the soles of my feet to be nibbled at by invisible herbivorous sea critters.

He told me to listen for the ocean inside the conch, and I heard waves pour into my brain like pasta into a colander. I wanted to tell him that I hated the ocean and that the sounds I was hearing were probably coming from the sea just a few feet away — much more believable than there being an entire body of water pooled within the small shell at my ear.

His hands were cold and smooth, unlike that curved evacuated-mollusc-hut which whistled waves into me. I held his hand against the shell for an uncomfortable amount of time. And, eventually, he left me holding it alone so that he could go and destroy the sandcastle of a girl he wouldn't admit to liking, all angsty-Godzilla-like, before plonking himself beside her — she rolled her eyes and played with her hair.

Alone, my hand warmed the conch, removing the lingering cold of his touch. I lowered it from my ear, however, I could still hear that ocean as I wandered home for dinner. As I walked, I kept turning back, half-expecting to see the entire ocean, sporting its various sea-life and boating debris, tip-toeing right behind me only to jump behind a lamppost in a Scooby-Doo-esque attempt at hiding.

I would come to drill a hole in it, the shell that is, through which to thread a piece of twine and hang from my neck.

Over the following years, the waves that poured into my ears by that conch never subsided, and I spent many wasted meals feeling seasick. I kept it from my parents, thinking it would pass — it was just a body of water after all, it had to shift at some point I thought. Sometimes it was a sonorous ebbing sloshing around the edges of my brain, and other times it was thunderous — as though of furious waves breaking against an ancient cliff's wearied shins.

School was difficult, as my head-bound waves would drown out the teacher's explanations of important mathematical principals, and I would be sent to the school nurse who jokingly said that she couldn't prescribe a dingy when I confessed to her what was happening. Word got around to the other kids, and beneath the waves in my ears I would hear mutterings and nicknames — a tittering aquifer for the waves in my head to ebb and flow along the top of, and sometimes beat against.

I could feel adrift anywhere. At any moment, the waves threatened to turn angry, and whether I were considering the price of branded pink-wafer biscuits in Tesco, queuing at a bar, or even on the toilet, I would suddenly feel marooned and desperate for a passing buoy or life-raft to cling to. I tried carrying a life raft around with me for a while, but people only stared.

I succumbed to sea-legs from time to time, and I didn't allow myself to drive in case I felt a strong wave buffet the inside of my skull, causing me to steer into oncoming traffic in anticipation of another wave. And once, on the 143 bus, I crumpled upon the floor when the swell was particularly strong, and clung to the nearest thing for safety — a pair of Nike 110s which irately kicked me in the teeth before I could explain that I had meant to grab the standing-passenger pole.

At university, a therapist called me delusional, but I told him he was delusional for wearing a double-breasted suit in the 2010s. I wasn't allowed back; and, apparently they're fashionable again, but I didn't know that.

Now, nearly two decades since that boy and his conch first poured waves towards my cochlea, an adult with emerging health complications and all, I stand once more on that same initial shore. The boy in me wants to look for sandy footsteps of the one who poured an ocean into my ear, but I haven't got the time for such childish things anymore.

I brought a kayak along, in which I cast off from this golden sand, struggling against the incoming tide. The conch which started this all sits in my lap — it had proven too cumbersome for a necklace.

Once fully on the water, with the shore barely visible behind me, I feel quietly at home, destination-less upon that unsteady mirror which rocks with the subtlety of candy floss. I let that long-vacant conch cup my ear, and I gaze at my watery reflection. I don't fully recognise the eyes; yet, they seem at home in that skull, as ripples distort wrinkles and waves pass through my forehead. I slip in, naked, to float with water filling my ears and bob as freely as a buoy unmoored.

And, now, floating aimlessly towards the horizon, the waves sound like a repeated soft splat and fizz of someone spilling Lilt onto a linoleum floor — I can hear my parents in the distance bemoaning the mess. The invisible anchors of childhood cut me loose somewhere along the way, bobbing towards the sunset; but, I cannot place exactly when.

PATRICK CLARKE IS A WRITER WHO HAS HAD WORK PUBLISHED IN THE LIKES OF THE MANCHESTER ANTHOLOGY FOR NEW WRITING AND AD ALTA: THE BIRMINGHAM LITERARY JOURNAL. SINCE COMPLETING AN MA IN CREATIVE WRITING AT THE UNIVERSITY OF MANCHESTER, PATRICK HAS BEEN WORKING AS A CONTENT WRITER WHILE ALSO WORKING ON A COLLECTION OF SHORT STORIES.

SHOW YOUR COLOURS

BY SARAH MCPHERSON

Pink for the party dress he chose for your daughter (a colour you hated); for the ham sandwiches you served up for afternoon tea; for the roses in the centerpiece, overturned on the grass.

Blue for the light cotton dress you wore that day; for the summer sky - pale in the morning, cobalt in the afternoon, midnight later; for his eyes, limpid and mournful when he confessed she had seen them together, and that she ran.

Yellow for the sun, burning the back of your neck as you searched for her; for the hearts of the daisies that had escaped the mower at the margins of your manicured lawn; for the faded shine of the ring on your third finger.

Orange for the sunset that gilded the horizon when you found her lying by the river; for the rust stain on the back of your friend's blouse that confirmed his betrayal; for the juice you poured with shaking hands the next morning, blindly following routine.

Red for the blood thumping in your temples, a drum solo only you can hear; for the paper heart coloured in childish crayon still stuck to the fridge, even now; for the lipstick stains you'd tried to ignore in the creases of his clothes.

Grey for the cloud that drifted over the sun as you poured drinks for the arriving guests and shrouded you in unexpected chill; for the iron strands in your hair that were not there before; for the shadow that will not leave your eyes or your heart.

SARAH MCPHERSON IS A SHEFFIELD-BASED WRITER AND POET, WITH WORK PUBLISHED IN ELLIPSIS ZINE, SPLONK, STORGY, THE CABINET OF HEED, AND ELSEWHERE. SHE HAS BEEN LONG/SHORTLISTED IN COMPETITIONS INCLUDING WRITERS' HQ, REFLEX FICTION AND CRANKED ANVIL, AND HAD A STORY SELECTED FOR BEST MICROFICTION 2021.

BLUE

BY JOHN BARRON

'There is no blue', she says. 'Not really'. She says this as she stirs her coffee, looking half at it and half at me, absent-mindedly encouraging entropy while the café mills around us, hardly noticing. I take the aversion of her gaze as a sign of indifference to me and, at that moment, the side of her cheek and the way a few strands of her hair fall past it, is the most beautiful thing I have ever seen. It's not until much later that I realise her eyes cannot meet mine for the same reason that I mentally beg with all my heart that they will. 'I mean, obviously there is a *blue* in your mind. And mine. But that's it, isn't it? In your mind?'

There are raised voices in the background, people ordering over the din of the cutlery and espresso machine hiss. A tour group, drawn by the wooden beams, aged-plaster walls, and the promise of the supernatural, shuffle through the door. Their guide prepares to wrap up for the evening before leaving them here to settle down with coffees and teas and a grateful proprietor friend. One final imagined scare before he can head home, his pocket jingling with appreciation.

'How do you mean?', I say, willing to play the fool just to hear her voice for a few seconds more.

'Nobody's blues are the same. Blue is no more than the mind's interpretation of a wavelength of a boson so powerful and mysterious it might as well be God,' (though God is not something she can bring herself to believe in, a source of many of our discussions through the years). 'Just a fleeting perspective from the smallest of windows onto an expanse of time and space so infinite as to make the very concept of either meaningless.' This is her point.

It is a response to my efforts to impress her when I explain what I do with my degree in chemistry, trying to match hers in physics.

'I can make you any colour you want,' I say at the time. 'I can make a blue like your eyes.'

'You can even dye my dress to match my eyes?'

'Exactly. Like, Dorothy.'

She smiles. Then a moment later she says that fateful line. It becomes the first of the many catchphrases that come to make up the language that only we share over time. 'There is no blue' one of us will say when the other comments on the blueness of the sky. 'There is no blue' when she picks blue for the colour of the walls of our first child's room. 'There is no blue' as I whisper how his eyes look on the monitor as he collects his degree.

The guide group gets closer now, threatening to drown out this perfect moment, because it is now, at this time, that I have that sudden feeling, like my heart is pulling at its tethers like a kite trying to escape a child's grasp. It is then I realise that this is the first time I have truly felt love, not its adolescent imitators or hope filled disappointments. It is a moment I want to last forever. That kite performs many different dances over the subsequent years, some in turbulent winds, some in depressive lulls, but it never stops. Until possibly that moment when I toss those symbolic tufts of earth over her last remains and brush the remaining grains off an age-leathered palm.

As the group approach, I try to ignore them, but at this distance I can't help noticing the peculiarity of their clothes. They are always dressed strangely and every year it seems to get more so.

'It's a bit like time.' She continues. And now I know this is her cue to try to put my field even further in its place.

'Blue, is like time?'

'Well, you know, it's not there, is it? Not physically there. Not as we think of it anyway.'

'Is that why you were late?'

She smiles again and the kite string almost breaks. Her tardiness is something that becomes less endearing, though ever-persistent, and is the source of our many petty arguments, pebbles in the mortar that cements us together. 'Past, future, now. They all happen at the same time. This moment isn't really happening. And yet it's always happening. And 'time' is just our brains' way of interpreting the inevitable decline of order. So, time is like blue.' And as she says that she takes a sip of the coffee she has been stirring and places it perfectly back down on the saucer with a finality of a judge's gavel. And that is that. Another of the universe's problems solved. Though she later retracts such certainty. Not that there is a later.

As her hand rests on the table, mine sidles across, unbid by any conscious part of me and a fingertip brushes against her thumb. It is not the first time we have touched, but somehow it is the most intimate and this moment, among infinite moments of now, is crystalised in time for me. She looks at me for the first time. I say something funny about the tour group whose backs are to us now. And she laughs. And the members of the group turn, some with a gasp, some with a scream, one or two bringing a hand to their chest. And then they laugh too, looking at the empty chairs and table that sit in front of them, not seeing us, because they never do, and laughing at themselves for believing in ghosts for the smallest of moments. The two time fragments pass each other: moth wings flitting by a night-darkened window. And then they turn away and applaud their leader as he bows and reminds them to tell their friends.

And I roll my eyes, indicating them to her. And she smiles once more and looks directly at me.

And her eyes are blue.

JOHN BARRON IS A TEACHER, GEEK AND OCCASIONAL WRITER. ONE DAY HE WOULD LOVE OTHER PEOPLE TO READ HIS WORK. HE LIVES IN LONDON WITH HIS WIFE AND CAT, TRYING HIS BEST TO BE A GOOD HUSBAND TO ONE AND FAITHFUL SERVANT TO THE OTHER. WHEN HE HAS FREE TIME AND ISN'T WRITING, HE LIKES TO DESIGN OR LEARN CODE. THIS RARELY HAPPENS.

THE FAVOURITE PLACE

BY G.A WOLF

Poinsettia kept watch. *I wonder who will come today?* Even though she had every opportunity to relish in the gorgeous watery blueness to her left, it was always far more intriguing to see what was happening to the right, where the land extended out for a few yards and then disappeared. She buzzed with excitement. She had no evidence something amazing was about to happen, it just felt that way.

The sky must have felt it too; it was shimmering and wide open with expectation and although it was far too early for the sun to show its full face, you could already feel the heat simmering. Grateful for the gentle light, the grass radiated bright green. The parts hidden by large rocks or sequestered by trees, looked on with jealousy.

Still hoping to snag Poinsettia's attention, the ocean spritzed onto the hill. A couple of crabs scurried from a hole and tried to make it safely into another, before someone snatched them up, or they got smashed by a careless foot. *Why don't they just stay put?* she thought, watching their attempts with bated breath.

Just as the last part of the crab's claw entered a sandy hole, a car arrived. 'Here we go,' whispered Poinsettia, bending slightly.

'Hmm, a sports car... and blood red... this should be interesting.'

She watched carefully as the car got closer and parked nearby. A man got out... judging by his highly tailored suit, he was not there to indulge in the sea. There was someone in the passenger seat, but it was difficult to tell who.

Damn. I wanna see. Poinsettia tried leaning out further but was constricted. She sighed. 'I guess I am gonna have to be patient with this one.'

Normally the cars that came *that* early in the morning were not luxury ones, more like station wagons, or those ones that were not necessarily *chic* but necessary. She always loved watching this one couple whose car was stuffed with sailing boards. They would bounce out of the shabby car, hoping that day would be the one when they conquered the waves like seasoned Olympians. A few hours later, when their muscles could no longer last against the watery beast, she felt their anguish, and sighed along with them.

It was a sheer treat to watch the old man arrive on his bicycle. Each time, there would be sweat trickling through the grooves in his face, and whatever shirt he was wearing, would be soaked from having to push his aged body up the gigantic hill that led to this prime location. Poised and calm, he'd strip off all his clothes, place them under a hibiscus bush and then ride off the cliff. The roar of the ocean was so loud, it was impossible to hear if he was okay. The next moments were always filled with both hope and dread, until the top of his bald head appeared as he climbed back up, put on his clothes, and then rode down the hill again.

The best moments were at first daylight, when a beautiful black woman would appear on foot, with a colourful bag over her shoulder and an equally colourful scarf wrapped around her head. She was always smiling and humming a tune. The melody reached the hill before she did. Once in her favourite spot, she'd pull a blanket out of the colourful bag and sit down. After reciting some sort of prayer, she would then open her mouth and sing. The most endearing sound rushed out and floated right over the ocean and up to the sun. It was always difficult for Poinsettia to hold back tears, as the song penetrated through her every fibre.

She paused. *I wonder where she is? ...it's been some time since she came*, thought Poinsettia, keeping watch of the well-dressed man in the red car.

Just as he was pulling out picnic chairs from the trunk, another car pulled up. The man turned and waved.

Excitement rushed through Poinsettia; it was always fun when someone new came, and now there were several new faces.

An elderly couple got out of the other car. Although dressed in bright colourful clothing, there was something sad about them. A sort of resigned sadness. Just as the woman started to walk towards the red car, the door to the passenger side flew open, and a little girl, dressed in a bright yellow dress popped out and went running to the woman.

'Grandma,' she screamed before throwing her arms open.

The older woman snatched her up into a long hug. 'Sarah.'

The fashionable men went over to the older man, who was now leaned up against his own car with his head bowed. With the picnic chairs in one hand, he locked his other arm into the old man's and pulled him off of the car. After hugging, they both started towards the ocean.

The little girl and the old woman did the same. Once all four had reached the base of the tree, the old woman took out a gold container from her bag.

'Can I say something first?' asked the little girl.

'Of course, my love…go ahead.'

The little girl took the jar and held it to her chest. 'Okay Mummy,' she said taking off the top of the jar. 'We are here at your favourite spot, under your favourite poinsettia tree, looking out to the sea.' She opened the jar and started dumping the contents.

A wave of warmth submerged into Poinsettia's roots. All of sudden she was filled with the same song the woman with the colourful scarf used to sing.

'Now you can rest in peace mummy,' said the little girl.

The group hugged.

'Mummy is gonna be so happy here… she can rest in this beautiful spot forever.'

'Yes baby,' said the man, mummy is good now.

Poinsettia watched, drenched with love.

THE FAVOURITE PLACES BY G.A WOLF © 2021.

G.A WOLF IS A 54-YEAR-OLD BLACK WOMAN WHO HAS DISCOVERED HER LOVE FOR WRITING. SHE HAS SPENT OVER 30 YEARS AS A SINGER, SONGWRITER AND PROFESSIONAL PERFORMER. SINCE COVID, SHE HAS COMPLETED A NOVEL, THE FAMOUS QUEEN NOBODY KNEW, AND SEVERAL SHORT STORIES.

SPENT MATCHES

BY TALIS ADLER

11/04/2020

Sarah,

I hope this email finds you well, and your sister too - I see you when you walk home from school most days and I wonder if you've noticed me striking matches down by the river. I got your email address from the teacher. I told her it was for a group assignment and I hope you don't mind me reaching out, but you walk past me a lot and you always look lost even though you're travelling the same path. You look like you need a friend.

Abby

22/04/2020

Sarah,

I hope this email finds you okay, you looked upset this morning and I don't remember the last time I saw your skin without bruises. Your little sister doesn't have any, but I think you know as well as I do that it's only a matter of time. I dropped my matches in the water yesterday when I saw your face. I used to be like you.

I think I can help.

Abby

26/04/2020

Sarah,

I know you're getting my emails because I saw you looking for me yesterday, but you didn't wave back. That's okay. You don't have to respond to my emails, but if you want me to keep sending them, just buy me a box of matches and leave it on the bench near the traffic lights on your walk home. If not, I'll stop bothering you. You still look lost.

Abby

28/04/2020

Sarah,

I hope this email finds you happier than the last time I saw you. Thank you for the matches, they were a good replacement for the ones I dropped. I'm still trying to dry those out but I don't think there's much point. You actually almost smiled at me yesterday, and I heard it's your birthday tomorrow but your dad's is on the same day. I'll buy a cake for your dad, maybe then he'll leave you alone.

Abby

29/04/2020

Sarah,

I hope this email finds you before your mother does, she looked angry when I brought over the cake with "stop hitting your daughter" iced into the white frosting. I'm lucky I got inside before she saw it. Your house is nicer than I expected, but you don't look comfortable in it. I saw the way you looked at the knife when I was cutting it, that familiar lost look, like you used to know the way out once but you've long since forgotten. There was a new bruise on your arm.

Abby

13/05/2020

Sarah,

I hope this email finds you healthy - you looked sick yesterday. I know you don't want to be at home, but you shouldn't keep coming to school if you're unwell. If you want, you can crash at mine; it's not the nicest place, but there's a lock on the door. You can bring your sister too.

Abby

18/05/2020

Sarah,

I hope this email finds you a tiny bit better than last week. Did you have fun at my place? I know you don't talk much and that's okay. Your sister seemed to have fun, so I hope that means you did too. I hope it's not too hard being back at home again. You look more and more lost on your walks home lately.

Abby

30/05/2020

Sarah,

I hope this email finds you safe. The teacher told me you passed out at school today. You've been wearing long sleeves and jeans for the last couple of weeks even though I'm sweating in skirts. She said she thought it was heat exhaustion. I think I know different - your dad's been getting worse, hasn't he? If you want my help, just say the word, or leave me a new pack of matches in the usual place if you don't feel like talking.

Abby

31/05/2020

Sarah

I hope this email finds you in the same place as your sister, and I hope that means you're far away from home. Thanks for the matches. Last time I brought a cake for your parents I forgot to light the candles.

Abby

01/06/2020

Sarah

I hope this email finds you less lost, wherever you are, and that you don't blame me too much for the fire that took your house. I really only meant to burn them, but fire is alive in a way that people aren't and it's always so much hungrier than I remember. It ate them too quickly.

Abby

02/06/2020

Sarah,

I hope this email finds you alive, despite the charred remains left in the bones of your house. I saw footprints in the ashes and I hope it was you or this was all for nothing. I sit by the river everyday, striking matches and dropping dead wood into the water, but I haven't seen you.

Abby

05/06/2020

Sarah,

I hope this email finds you on the run from the law, and I'm sorry you were blamed for the premeditated murder of your parents in a mysterious house fire that only you survived. It was lucky your sister was at a friend's house, but I suppose that means you're separated now. I hope you're not lost anymore, that at least when you're running you know where you're headed.

Abby

03/07/2020

Sarah,

I hope this email finds you safe, wherever you are. I'm running out of damp matches to strike but I don't want to use the ones you bought me because they're all I've got left of you since I burned down your house. Your sister came over to say goodbye yesterday, apparently she's going into a good home so maybe something positive did come of all this mess I caused.

Abby

17/08/2020

Sarah,

I hope this email finds you. I miss you. I only wanted to help.

Abby

31/10/2020

Sarah,

I hope this email finds you. I miss you. I only wanted to help.

Abby

24/11/2020

Sarah,

I hope this email finds you. I miss you. I only wanted to help.

Abby

01/01/2021

Sarah,

Thanks for the matches.

Abby

TALIS ADLER IS A RECENT GRADUATE OF THE UNIVERSITY OF WORCESTER, WHERE SHE RECEIVED A FIRST IN JOINT HONOURS DEGREE IN CREATIVE AND PROFESSIONAL WRITING, AND SCREENWRITING. WHILE STUDYING, SHE CO-STARTED THE POETRY SOCIETY AT HER UNIVERSITY, AND SHE IS CURRENTLY COLLATING HER FINAL YEAR POETRY PROJECT, WHICH SHE AIMS TO PLACE WITH A PUBLISHER FOLLOWING HER DEGREE.

SHE HAS HAD HER WORK PUBLISHED IN THE MARCH ISSUE OF SMALL LEAF PRESS'S MAGAZINE AND IN PUBLICATIONS ONLINE. SHE IS THE ASSISTANT EDITOR OF DEAR READER POETRY.

PART 3

Now you see me.

NOW YOU DON'T...

BY HAZEL OSMOND

THIRD PLACE WINNER

They used to laugh about it before they went on. It was their warm-up and lucky routine.

She'd be contorting herself in some corner near the plug socket, coaxing her hair to twice its volume with a hot wand, and he'd take *his* wand out of its case and with a white, black, white wave over his baldness, command, 'Abracadabra, give me a full head of curls.'

She'd wait a couple of beats before saying, 'Not working, love. You tried putting a plug on it?'

She hadn't minded how scruffy the dressing rooms were, although she didn't like it so much when they had to share with other acts. Some of the men ... well ... you wouldn't take your coat off in front of them. She kept hoping he'd tell everyone to get lost for half an hour while she changed, but it was always her heading to the loo with her frock and tiara.

'You've been getting yourself sawn in half for five years,' he'd say. 'How hard can it be to wrestle yourself into a dress in the toilet cubicle?'

Those were the glory days - she understands that now. She was in love with him and with standing on a stage and waiting for the curtains to draw back. Felt drunk on the sound of the applause; hugged by the warm lights.

She could read the signs of a shiny, bright future in

the way the rhinestones on her bodice sparkled; how he seemed broader and taller in his suit.

'Did you see that audience?' he'd say, as they came off stage. 'Had them in the palm of my hand - open mouthed, eyes out on stalks. And that 'Ooh' when I chopped open the apple and the diamond ring fell out. We can go all the way, I'm telling you. All the way.'

She didn't mention the teenagers who looked bored; the old guy having a kip at the back of the stalls.

Now and again, she'd ask if she could do a couple of the tricks herself; she knew them well enough.

'It'll just confuse the punters,' he said. 'Let me do the magic. You do the pretty.'

Most of the time she didn't mind. She loved to watch his hands when he was working, the graceful flourishes and spins. The shuffles and mis-direction. Funny, really, because at home anything that called for dexterity, he struggled with - painting the skirting board without getting gloss on the wall; knocking in a nail.

Touching her exactly how she liked to be touched.

On stage though, like a fish in water or a bird in the sky, he was in his element. A Master of Illusion.

Rope tricks, coins pulled from amazed ears; levitation, the lady sawn in half, and, for the climax, two doves conjured out of a burning pan.

He loved those doves. Would get them out of their cage to perch on his finger. Blew gently on their breast feathers. Insisted on feeding them by hand.

'If I was the jealous type …' she'd say and pretend it was a joke because it was easier than thinking about how hard he could be on her if she missed a cue, or put on a few extra pounds.

The venues got smaller and the digs, shoddier. Their names slid down the bill. They were beaten in TV-inspired talent shows by young kids with unreliable voices, but tear-inducing back stories.

One night they went on before a troupe of male strippers, and he came off stage fuming at the stuff the women had shouted at him.

'It's just a bit of fun,' she said in the dressing room and he pushed her so hard she stumbled and turned her ankle. In A&E he entertained the nurses by pulling cotton wool balls from their ears.

She went back to working full-time and he diversified into children's parties. Gave it up after their own kids were born because he didn't have the patience – it was only a matter of time before a birthday boy or girl got backhanded.

She realised it was curtain down, lights out when she found the dove cage out in the wheelie bin.

'Where are the doves?' she'd asked, but he didn't answer.

Now *she's* the one conjuring up illusions.

She holds his hand when they are out together. Smiles at her mother and tells her everything is fine.

Pulls the wand from the tube of concealer and dabs it on her bruises. Makes them disappear before the kids wake up.

NOW YOU DON'T... BY HAZEL OSMOND © 2021.

HAZEL OSMOND LIVES IN NORTHUMBERLAND AND WRITES SHORT STORIES, FLASH FICTION AND HAS HAD FOUR ROMANTIC COMEDIES PUBLISHED BY QUERCUS. HER FLASH FICTION HAS

BEEN SHORTLISTED AND LONGLISTED IN THE BATH FLASH FICTION AWARD AND SHORTLISTED IN THE HASTINGS LITERARY FESTIVAL.

DANDELION & THE TRAPEZE EVENT

BY NIAMH MAC CABE

'I'm gone to seed,' I answer. You would've got it straight-away.

They rephrase. No place for an elderly lady, blah blah, we're prepared to see the original offence as an accident, an uncharacteristic... did they say un-characteristic *mishap*? Passion, youth, we're open to expressions of regret, please reconsider, etcetera. The usual dross, their soulful doggy-eyes darting between me and the in-house psychiatrist. Or are those my pendulum eyes left-right-left-right-blink-left-right.

Re-phrase. Re-gret. Re-consider.

I inhale, crack the thick knuckles you said you loved. Re-ply.
'Thank you for the opportunity. When opening a door, one pushes on the spot furthest from the hinges. Pushing closer requires more force. Although the work done is the same, people generally prefer to apply less force, hence the location of the door handle,

the one, for example, currently pointing at my back. But thank you all very much. Very kind.'

Then before shuffling out in my beloved and ancient Birkenstock Men's slippers: 'To be clear: elderly or not, I'd do it all again, if the whoring bitch were alive enough to have it done to her. May ye have a lovely, lovely day.'

I've returned unopened the Board's every suggestion, however torqued their sugary phrasing at these annual summonings. I've dodged the carefully-considered alightments of the psychiatrist's coughs. Because both you and I know the truth lies close to the hinges; I'd rather persist in this place than be unfaithful to our glorious trapeze event. Sleep well, my love. It's you who is seeding, laid out in your sparkling aerial costume, your dainty white calves corseted in heel-less, toe-less leatherette boots, am I right? And the stout rooted dandelions ticking their gossamer clock-seeds skyward every year over your headless grave; I've seen them in my dreams, made wine with their golden flowers, gulped it down to quench this god-awful thirst.

No. I'll continue with the group art sessions and their gaudy landscapes, their fat yellow flowers. I'll continue with helping in the airless canteen, plastic-gloved, masked. I'll continue featuring in documentaries, my palsied hands sought out. Of course I'll not recant, you can rest easy on that. Oh please, they'll beg, don't give in, you've so much more life to live, so much more!

I don't know if that's true, hope to God it's not.

Walk me back to our starlit youth; to that dazzling night under the canvas dome; knowing he's in the audience, knowing he's here to watch you, his secret

little sweetheart in your glittering gold costume
with our intertwined initials hand-embroidered over
the heart by me, by my very own strong and nimble
fingers, remember? I'll start over, and I promise you
I'll do it all again. I'll hold out my hands to you, I'll
unfurl my chalked fingers, the ones you know well,
the ones you've come to rely on. You'll reach for them,
and at the last moment, upside-down on our twisting
trapeze pendulum, his eyes upon your gilded, your
trickster, your treacherous body, I'll swing these
hands away and watch you, my flower, fall.

NIAMH MAC CABE IS AN AWARD-WINNING WRITER, PUBLISHED
IN MANY JOURNALS AND ANTHOLOGIES INCLUDING NARRATIVE
MAGAZINE, THE STINGING FLY, MSLEXIA, SOUTHWORD, WASAFIRI,
NO ALIBIS PRESS, THE IRISH INDEPENDENT, THE LONDON
MAGAZINE, AESTHETICA, THE LONELY CROWD, LIGHTHOUSE,
STRUCTO, BARE FICTION, TEARS-IN-THE-FENCE, AND THE BRISTOL
PRIZE ANTHOLOGY. SHE'S BEEN TWICE NOMINATED FOR A
PUSHCART PRIZE, SELECTED FOR THE BEST BRITISH & IRISH
FLASH FICTION LIST, NOMINATED FOR BEST SMALL FICTIONS,
AND AWARDED A TYRONE GUTHRIE CENTRE RESIDENCY. SHE
LIVES WITH HER SONS IN RURAL LEITRIM, IRELAND.

SOMEONE LIKE YOU

BY CLARE MARSH

Max, my booking agent, rang this morning to deliver the bombshell. 'Have you seen the latest photo on Instagram?'

'What photo?'

'Of your tribute act.'

It takes a minute to realise he doesn't mean me but you, my alter ego, Adele. 'And?'

'It's all over social media. She doesn't look the same.'

'Why? Has she had plastic surgery?'

'No, but you still wouldn't recognise her.'

'Because..?'

'She's lost seven stone and could be a completely different person.'

Of course I'd seen the photos on Instagram last Christmas when you'd lost some weight – but I could still delude myself we were just about in the same ball-park back then. You hadn't posted many photos since.

'Shit. But at least I'm not a look-alike, or body double.'

'No, Sam, your vocals might get you through temporarily, but when the public get used to seeing Adele's new image, especially with her latest album coming out soon, you'll be irrelevant. Please tell me you haven't been piling on yet more pounds at home during lockdown?'

My silence was the only answer Max needed.

'Look, if you want to do those next three bookings after Christmas you'll have to radically adjust and update your appearance. There are other singers who would be a better 'fit' now – with fit, not fat, being the operative word on so many levels.'

'Ouch. That's hard – not to say outright rude.'

'It's meant to push you into action.'

'I thought body image didn't matter nowadays – whatever happened to no fat shaming?'

'Tell that to the celebs. Adele was a rarity – a confident, world class musician who just happened to be on the larger side – and now same talent, different size.'

Lockdowns have devastated my performance business. I still do my daily vocal practice, with backing tracks, in the living room. Our neighbours, working from home at present, must be sick to death of hearing the same repeated repertoire. I haven't been as diligent, though, in following any minimal exercise routine, instead a short walk to pick up essentials (mostly snacks) from the corner shop has been my limit. To be honest, I've been comfort eating, like much of the population. The bathroom scales show their highest ever reading. Mum's always been 'a feeder', most probably that's what started the problems in the first place. She's been baking cakes like someone possessed. I've kept saying I'll get to grips with my weight once 'this is all over'.

The issues started early. I went from being called 'chubby' by dad, to being bullied at school and my response was to eat more desperately. My physique then made me useless at sports, so I'd hide in my room, where my outlet was listening to the radio and singing along for hours on end. You became my role model, Adele, and you were like the big sister I never had. One day Mum overheard me belting out one of your songs.

'Sam, you sound just like her – why you almost look like her, with the right clothes and make up!'

Something clicked in my brain – at last I'd found something I was good at and how to be me. There was a talent show in school and I entered. Nothing lost if I failed as I was about to leave anyway. But that wasn't how it panned out. My set went down a storm as I gave your songs my all. Afterwards even those who'd mocked me previously were impressed and I felt vindicated. I took a boring day job in an insurance office, leaving evenings and weekends free. I successfully auditioned for the Stars4Hire Agency, signed up with Max and the work started 'rolling in', to quote you. I enjoyed copying your hairstyles and those black lace dresses suited me nearly as well as they did you. I learned how to do your trademark eyeliner flick and simulated your enviable high cheekbones by artful contouring, then shaded in your cute chin dimple. Performing as you was like slipping on the protective armour of your persona, and was the only time I felt positive about myself. On stage, I accepted my plus size and realised it was an advantage.

Over the next years, I worked up to more prestigious venues, coat-tailing on your meteoric career and classic repertoire. My reviews were excellent: 'authentic, passionate vocals', 'professional and sings with genuine emotion' and, after a memorable outdoor event, 'Sam set fire to the rain despite the downpour mid set'.

But maybe complacency crept in about my looks and health. I've had plenty of time to think while I've been furloughed by the government. Being overweight is a risk for developing Covid-19. I'd already decided to get a grip before I saw this photo today taken on your 32nd birthday. You look simply stunning, girlfriend! I've just checked out the diet you followed. I don't like the sound of all the green juices you drink, but I'm pleased that you can still enjoy dark chocolate and red wine. So I've decided to stick with those two and skip the juice. I plan to take things a whole lot slower than you did.

Strange how lockdown has changed everything. The local music scene has blossomed via Zoom and now I sing as myself instead of impersonating you. A group, who're big on the club circuit, had just lost their lead singer, they saw a clip of me and asked me to join them. I didn't hesitate.

Now, like you, I'm setting out on a new stage in my musical career. I owe you so much for the confidence you've given me in accepting who I am and I'll always admire you. When I perform cover versions of your iconic songs in future it will be me singing, instead of me pretending to be you. I'll work on new music, maybe write some of my own – at least it will give the neighbours a change.

'Dinner's ready, Samuel,' Mum calls from downstairs. 'It's your favourite.'

SOMEONE LIKE YOU BY CLARE MARSH © 2021.

CLARE MARSH LIVES IN WEST KENT AND IS AN INTERNATIONAL ADOPTION SOCIAL WORKER. SHE WRITES POETRY, FLASH FICTION AND SHORT STORIES. A PREVIOUS WINNER OF THE SENTINEL ANNUAL SHORT STORY COMPETITION, HER WRITING HAS APPEARED IN MANY PLACES. SHE WON THE 2020 OLGA SINCLAIR PRIZE (NORWICH WRITERS' CIRCLE). SHE WAS

AWARDED M.A. CREATIVE WRITING (UNIVERSITY OF KENT) IN 2018 AND NOMINATED FOR A USA PUSHCART PRIZE IN 2017.

A DRAG QUEEN NAMED LIPSTIK

BY CONOR DUGGAN

I

Little Jesse struts into the living room in front of his aunts, wearing his mother's race day hat. The purple plume bobs from side to side as he goes.

'Take that off right now,' shouts his embarrassed mother.

Jesse, with his hands on his hips, turns and addresses his audience, 'She's only angry because she knows it looks *way* better on me'. Everybody starts laughing. His mother's furious.

Then he walks over to the backdoor like an actor leaving the stage, and adds, 'Besides, mother always says I should wear a hat outdoors,' before disappearing out into the sunshine.

II

He hears footsteps coming up the stairs and panics. He stands petrified on a stool beside his mother's dressing table, a tube of lipstick between his fingers.

She's coming. He jumps off the stool and runs into her en-suite.

'Is that you Jesse?' his mother calls out.

With tissue paper held to his nose, he runs out past her to the other bathroom at the end of the hall.

'It's just a nosebleed,' he yells.

The door now locked, he lowers the tissue and looks in the mirror. His face is smudged with red as though he's just eaten Spaghetti Bolognese.

His mother stands worriedly by the dressing table. *That's the third nose bleed this month*, she thinks. She glances at the mirror on the table and notices it's been angled downwards. She sighs, and then silently adjusts it back to its normal position.

III

Thud, thud, thud. Scrunched paper balls bounce off Jesse's head. The boys behind him snigger. He picks them up and collects them in a pile on his desk. They remain unopened, the messages buried inside.

He takes out a needle and thread from his pencil case, and carefully feeds the thread through the paper balls. When it's ready, he ties it around his neck, swivels around to the boys behind him, and says, 'If you boys keep giving me pearls, I'm gonna make a necklace'.

IV

His parents didn't recognise him when they walked past: that's how good his makeup was. He leaned against a lamppost to steady himself, his heart palpitating. He had thought they were away for the weekend. His anxieties became liquid, and began to soak through his skin. They passed out of view, and he ran into the nearest restaurant, and puked so violently he collapsed into a perfumed mess around the restroom sink.

V

Dad's found out.

Jesse hadn't realised the veranda had been re-painted. It was mostly dry, yet the stilettos left their impressions as he came home during the night. His father was mortified when he found out the imprints on the front steps were of his son's 'lady shoes'. He skipped work, and spent the day sanding and repainting the wood before anyone else saw.

But when he found the suitcase full of dresses under the bed, it was too much. Jesse was out.

VI

Jesse steps out of the taxi and his stilettos shatter the midnight puddles of downtown Sydney like sequined lightning bolts. He goes into the club: Showtime. The crowd have been waiting, but he doesn't care; he comes onstage with a presence that silences all murmurs of his delay. His outfit is almost complete: golden curls, a necklace of pearls, and a wavy hat. Complete except for lipstick, which he puts on last.

He steps up to the microphone, and pauses. *She's furious, she sighs, they snigger, he's mortified.* He's learned to let it go. The crowd wait in silent anticipation as he withdraws a tube of lipstick concealed in his hat; his trademark move.

He applies it in one smooth oval, and pressing his lips to the microphone, he whispers the refrain that sends his audience wild: *'If you boys keep giving me pearls, I'm gonna make a necklace'.*

CONOR DUGGAN IS A GEOLOGIST WHO HAS TURNED
HIS ATTENTION TO CREATIVE WRITING. HE WRITES FLASH
FICTION, POETRY, AND LIMERICKS. HE IS ALSO ENJOYS
BOTANY. CURRENTLY STUDYING PROSE FICTION AT UEA.

THE LONGEST DAY

BY SUSAN WIGMORE

I know something is up when I find your Elvis costume laid out on the bed in June. Las Vegas circa 1970, especially made, your design. You run your hand over its fringes and beads, the effortless grace of its hip-slung belt. When the charity shops re-open, you'll take it to Oxfam, you say. You'll eat your hat if Porthcawl happens this year, and you've lost so much weight, it would look as if it were hanging from a broomstick anyway. Besides. You've had a message from a woman named Angie. You pause. I wait.

– Porthcawl, last year. It didn't mean anything. In fact, there wasn't even an 'it' to speak of. You didn't want to come.

– Couldn't come. Remember?

And I wait some more. She worked for the local news programme, had to cover the biggest gathering of Elvis acts this side of Graceland and wanted to do a piece on you, the geography teacher's take on the King. She'd seen your Polk Salad and loved it.

– I bet she did, I say, and wonder why she got in touch with you all these months later.

– Perhaps it's that need to make sure people you know are all right, you say, reading my mind. You know, in times of war, an act of terrorism, a state of national emergency —

You look pale so I tell you to stop talking, though I may not phrase it quite like this.

Then I remember what the doctors said about building up your strength gradually.

– We'll try another walk tomorrow, I say. It's the summer solstice. And we'll have more chance of dodging people if we go early.

I persuade you that a man who can wow a crowd, and at least one journalist, with his Polk Salad Annie can manage early. Because I want – more than anything I've ever wanted – to show you what I love about the world. A rediscovery, when you were so ill and I was so lonely, of something I'd lost along the way. The Elvis costume goes back into the spare room.

As we set off next morning, the sun dresses up the sky in its sunrise colours. The air swells with the scent of honeysuckle, earth glutted with last night's rain. You fuss with the zip on your fleece and tut a robin from a crab apple tree.

– You're like that horse in the field over there, I say. What would it take for him to lift his head from the grass?

– A full stomach, you say. And zip yourself up against the chill.

Scones from yesterday, baked in celebration of flour appearing in the supermarket, are in my pocket as a picnic breakfast. Now they seem inadequate and heavy, like a clumsy joke.

– I read a story once, I say, about a woman who was using some super-duper glue. The box said it was so good you could stick yourself to the ceiling with it.

– Nobody believes stuff like that.

– Her husband rubbished it too.

– I rest my case.

– And then he came home one night and found her hanging upside down from the ceiling by the soles of her shoes.

We walk for a while without speaking. I run a hand across ears of wheat, and say, listen. You stop, hands in pockets, fleece pulled up around your ears. I see the newly familiar air pockets at the knees and buttocks of your joggers.

– Today's the day the sun stands still, I say. You sigh and tell me that it's always spinning. And then:

– What happened to the woman on the ceiling?

– Her husband glued himself next to her and they hung there together.

You laugh.

– Romantic, isn't it? I say.

And I watch swifts there and gone against clouds, a spider climbing the air between leaves on an ancient ash, a breeze chasing itself through long grass. I close my eyes.

Then, from the unruliness of oxeye daisies gracing the field's margins, a hare. Leaping for no other reason it seemed than it could.

– Did you see that? you say. Pure energy. Amazing.

There is nothing I can think of to say so I take your hand. Clouds bank around a gash of sun; the sky moves slowly. For a moment we stand, held by surface tension.

You touch my arm. There are dog-walkers on the far side of the field and a runner weaving through trees; it's not worth the risk. Anyway, it's time to head back. You fancy a drink. We could start a new box set, polish off those scones. Who cares if it's only six in the morning? Life couldn't get much stranger. I smile and you tell me I'm ineffable. I ask what that means. You know it's something big and important but can't get much beyond this. We can look it up later, you say.

Your step is steadier on the path now, and as we walk towards home, you begin to whistle. It's an old Elvis song I haven't heard for ages, so it takes a while for me to place it. Then it comes to me: 'Stuck on You'. And I just can't shake it off.

THE LONGEST DAY BY SUSAN WIGMORE © 2021.

SUSAN WIGMORE RETIRED FROM TEACHING IN 2018, AND COMPLETED THE UNDERGRADUATE DIPLOMA IN CREATIVE WRITING AT THE UNIVERSITY OF OXFORD LAST YEAR. SHE HAS BEEN EXPERIMENTING WITH DIFFERENT GENRES OF WRITING EVER SINCE, AND — WRITER'S BLOCK NOTWITHSTANDING —HAS BEEN ENJOYING THE WHOLE CREATIVE PROCESS IMMENSELY.

RULES FOR BOYS AT PLAY

BY ERIK WIJKSTRÖM

It had been building for some time now, this creeping rivalry, this petty sniping. Did they really think he wouldn't notice? Little fools! It had gone too far; he could smell it festering like the foul air from the changing rooms. The creases on Miyagi's furrowed brow deepen. Outside, trees bend for cover in the school yard and the wind thrusts against the tall windows of the dojo. Distracted by the force of the weather, Geneva's head karate trainer looks out. They would come soon, the parents, eager to gather their offspring for a weekend in the mountains, to escape the rain for the snow. He must fix this. Now.

He folds his arms, letting air flow between pursed lips.

Slowly, he turns to face the youths.

The *karate-ka* move uneasily.

A decision is overdue.

Yet, he hesitates.

There is something in the dynamic between the two teens that short-circuits him. He looks at Nicolas, the dark one: body tense like a bowstring, toes clenching the tatami, the floor mat, so that it squeaks almost rhythmically. He thinks of a pacing panther. How old could he be now, fourteen? Hair and eyes black as the gathering night, movements like something out of the wild, feline almost; no awkwardness anywhere, no body part playing catch-up; puberty had been kind. Still a child, yes, he thinks, but the childishness is long gone.

Yet so much fury inside.

Unsettled, Miyagi folds his hands behind his back and steps around the boys. He sees how they strain to follow, how they wish they could swivel their heads like owls. The other one, Paul, a year older perhaps: a blond Viking - flashing ways, easy charm and confidence. Sunshine radiating from every pore, strutting like a stork. Life on a platter. Careful. He should not show prejudice. Miyagi shakes his head. The boys' trajectories had been set on course for collision from day one, but this is not a case of bullied and bully. Both exude physical presence: two alphas; so different, yet so similar. If they only knew.

His eyes fall on Nicolas's brown bracelet, a band of woven leather ever- present on the boy's wrist. In a flash he knows what to do. Risky. But simple. There is something comical about the way they stand before him now as he comes full circle, their expressions equalised in shared expectation. Antagonism gone and childishness back, as if seeking guidance and closure. This is what the world needs now, he thinks: a judge for boys at play. Rules and structure. He finds himself trying to suppress a smile and realizes that the unusual contortion of his face has them looking perplexed.

He gestures to the middle of the tatami and barks, '*Randori!*'

133

'But –'

'What –'

'Enough! You want to mess around, be tough? Big boys, right? So, you do it proper, not behind my back, if...,' he raises a finger. '*If* I see *one* drop of blood – you not come back here, ever. Show respect, like always. Bow before, bow after - no different. Understand?'

The boys nod.

He backs away, satisfied, thumping the Toyota-red tatami with his right heel for emphasis. The rest of the class retreats so that the boys are encircled.

It starts slow and tentative, but Paul is soon all but dancing around Nicolas, light footed, quick - calibrating, testing. Miyagi knows that the younger boy is less comfortable with the free *randori* style, that he is better at the structured, defined exercises, the *katas* – where moves are choreographed, predictable and precise. But then there is that catlike quality.

Miyagi finds himself holding his breath.

Something in Nicolas's expression, the fire in his eyes, brings back that first day: a frail, skinny form – elbows poking in all directions, hiding the dirty brown bracelet in the stubborn fold of his arms. Refusing to take it off; his still-too-large kimono with the stiff ends of the white belt sticking out like a pair of extra arms. Miyagi had tried to explain in his pitiful French: *ça va pas,* he could not wear anything, no necklaces, earrings, rings... he kneeled, it could break, he said, get caught, rip – or worse – hurt someone. The boy left, just like that. And then, the following day, the father's sincere and apologetic explanation and the boy's equally sincere mortification at his own father's words. It had been his mother's, the father had explained, he never took it off - not even in the shower.

Miyagi had wanted to ask more but resisted and then relented.

A sudden movement.

A shout so sharp, so ear-piercingly clear and unexpected that the circle of *karate-ka* stager back in unison. Paul is flat on his back, wide-eyed with Nicolas on top. Miyagi is thunderstruck. Nicolas has never uttered the *kiai* cry. Not once. And this despite Miyagi's insistence – even taunting, in his weaker moments. This had been the reason Miyagi had not let him advance in grade. And now this masterstroke.

'*Yame!*' Miyagi has to lift Nicolas off, holding him by the collar like a kitten torn from its prey while he waves at the others to line up. When Paul hesitates, Miyagi pulls him back and, with a bead of sweat between his eyes, manoeuvres the boys so they stand shoulder to shoulder. Outside a line of parents has formed, hoods snapping in the wind. For two long seconds the silence is complete.

Finally, Miyagi grunts, 'Your belt!'

Nicolas stares, motionless. But Paul understands; he turns to Nicolas and, with a quick glance, unties his belt, folds it and hands it to Miyagi who walks away and returns with a new one that he gives Paul. Paul tears off the wrapping and ties the new, stiff brown belt around Nicolas's waist so firmly that the boy wobbles.

The two brown belts stand with Miyagi between them.

And there it is, finally. A glint of recognition.

A subtle change in poise.

A shift in trajectory.

They bow.

ERIK WIJKSTRÖM WORKS FOR AN INTERNATIONAL ORGANISATION IN GENEVA, SWITZERLAND. BORN IN INDIA, HE GREW UP IN AFRICA AND ITALY - BUT HE FEELS MOST AT HOME IN THE FORESTS OF SWEDEN, HIS "HOME" COUNTRY.

FLASHES

BY CONOR MONTAGUE

A flash: a thump to the back of his head. Ed sinks into a warm viscous flow as it slurps into a chasm. He teeters on the edge, slowly rolls over. Eyes jolt open. He's spewed from the chasm. Blinding glare. Tang of singed enamel. A voice from above. Silhouette.

ONE!

An operating theatre: masked surgeon in a bright halo. Ed battles the anaesthetic, fears sinking, fears nothing. The Andaman Sea. Their honeymoon. Ascending towards surface glare. His measured breaths. Drone of engines through water. Silhouette overhead: a distant voice.

TWO!

Flashes. Countless flashes. White sparks swirl into black. *Inis Meáin*: Summer '96. Stargazing by the cliffs. Gannets honk above. Waves thunder onto rocks below. Next stop, America. A fighter could do well there. If he had it in him. A figure stands over him.

THREE!

It's a referee. He's down. Head anchor-heavy on canvas, which seems adrift on the swells west of Aran.

The stinging jibes at the press conference. 'Do you think a man of your age can withstand the power of Tiger Lopez?' Flashes. Cameras shooting. Shooting. recording his frailty.

FOUR!

Ed rolls onto his right shoulder, swivels onto one knee. The gym in Brockton: Goody beside him on the apron. 'Always take the count, son. If you're hurt, take the count.' A commentator spews into a microphone. 'He's down... Ed Joyce, the Man of Aran, is down in the first round here in Madison Square Garden. Tiger Lopez has one hand on the featherweight title.'

FIVE!

Ed runs into the dawn. Heaves icy air into deprived lungs. Vapour exhalations merge into the fingers of mist reaching up from the valley. He wills burning legs up steep slope. Goody's voice: 'Your pegs gotta be independent, son. When your brain is mush and your senses all fucked-up, your pegs need to stand alone.'

SIX!

A blood-speckled white shirt. Roar of the crowd. Stench of sweat and blood and leather. Punching the heavy bag as Goody preaches: 'You think they gonna hand you that title? No siree, you gotta grab that motherfucka... No doubt.' The mantra beats through the gym in time with the combinations. 'No doubt. We ain't got no doubt.'

SEVEN!

An overhand right. Caught cold. Careless. Slow bringing back the jab. Ed looks to his corner. Flash of Goody's crooked smile. That was Tiger's best shot. They both know it. Tiger poised across the ring. Eyes ablaze with the desire to demolish a legend in front of the world. Ed shifts weight onto his left leg. Pushes off his knee.

EIGHT!

The arena erupts with his rise. The referee wipes gloves on shirt. 'You alright, Ed?' The arena swirls around three referees. 'Never been better.' A bellow from the corner: 'No doubt!' Ed inhales Goody's conviction with the bays of the mob. The referee shouts 'Box!' The arena soars toward crescendo. Tiger Lopez bolts into focus.

FLASHES BY CONOR MONTAGUE © 2021.

CONOR MONTAGUE IS AN IRISH WRITER WORKING IN LONDON. A GRADUATE OF THE MA IN WRITING AT THE NATIONAL UNIVERSITY OF IRELAND GALWAY, HE HAS PUBLISHED IN SHORT FICTION, CREATIVE NON-FICTION AND ACADEMIA. MOST RECENTLY WITH REFLEX FICTION, FLASH 500, TSS FLASH 400, LONDON INDEPENDENT STORY PRIZE, THE WRITERS BUREAU SHORT STORY COMP 2019, BRAY LITERARY FESTIVAL FLASH FICTION COMP 2019, THE BRIDPORT PRIZE 2019, THE FISH FLASH FICTION PRIZE 2020, BANGOR LITERARY JOURNAL FORTY WORDS COMP 2020, STRANDS INTERNATIONAL FLASH FICTION COMPETITION 2020, V.S. PRITCHETT SHORT STORY PRIZE 2020 AND HAMMOND HOUSE INTERNATIONAL LITERARY PRIZE 2020. CONOR ALSO WRITES FOR STAGE AND SCREEN.

THE WISH

BY KEVIN WEST

Hey, buddy, can you spare a dollar?

No.

Ok. Sorry. Maybe spare a penny then for a hungry mate?

No.

No? Can't spare a copper penny?

I said no.

Well, here's a penny for you, then, buddy.

I don't want a penny.

I'm very sorry that you don't even have a penny to spare. I guess you're down on your luck, and hey, I know how it goes, so here's a penny for you.

I said I don't want your penny.

I want you to have it, buddy. I really do.

I don't want it, buddy.

Ok. Here's a dollar.

I don't want your dollar either, *buddy*.

It's my last dollar but I really think you need it more than I do so please take it.

I said I don't want your fucking *dollar*.

But it's the least I can do for a fellow human who's having a rough time. And what's a dollar to me? I mean, it's all I have, that's what it is to me, but what is it in the grand scheme of things? It's not worth mentioning, that's what it is. It's the least I can do.

I don't want it. Go away.

Please take it.

I said I don't fucking want it!

Where are you going?

Leave me the fuck alone!

I'm just trying to help you out, man.

You're not helping me out, man!

Well, I'm sorry about that. I detected a certain profound level of destitution in your inability to spare a penny for a fellow sufferer and so I thought I would step in and attempt to turn the tide in your favor with a small, admittedly, but nonetheless significant, hopefully, contribution to the cause, if you know what I'm saying. But I'm sorry if I have misapprehended the situation. I'll turn away, then, with my dollar still in my possession, still clutched in my grip, if you are not desirous to have it.

Why did you ask me for a dollar?

Pardon me?

Why did you ask me for a dollar earlier if you already had one?

Well, yes, I had one but, you see, I desired another one.

You were being greedy.

Is that not the way of the world, sir—requited desire causing greater desire?

You were being selfish.

Guilty as charged. And upon gaining the second, I then would have ratcheted up to the next level of selfishness and desired a third and fourth on top of that, and with instant ferociousness. Is this not the case for nearly all human beings, as we are, after all, monstrously alike?

You were being greedy and selfish, and also, in a sense, misrepresenting your poverty as greater than mine when mine, I believe, is greater than yours since I don't have even a single penny on my person, having disposed of all my spare (so to speak) change, in the fountain in the town square where one can make a wish by tossing in coins.

You disposed of all your coins in the fountain in the town square?

Yes, I dispossessed myself of all my gold into that very fountain because it is the nearest thing that we have to a wishing well around these parts.

And what, pray tell, did you wish so fervently that you would use up every last golden coin in pursuit of it?

Of that I will not speak.

You will not speak of your most fervent wish?

I will not speak of it in public to a stranger, no I will not. I'll not speak of my wish nor slander my sorrow nor idle my time away in the gossip of gain and loss.

Slander your sorrow? Now you've piqued my curiosity with such language! Yet will you say nothing of this matter?

Nothing. The only wish I will speak of, sir, is my wish for you to pass on.

To pass on, eh? To ignore the slight that has just been delivered to me by a stranger in a way that could be described as casually cruel? Is that what you wish?

No slight was intended, sir. It is no sign of disrespect to wish to be left alone, for that is my only wish, that is my most fervent wish, and one that is worth going broke over, aye, one that is worth spending all one's wealth on to attempt to prevent an eternal sojourn in the land of the damned, if you know what I mean; the hot place!

What are you saying, sir? Your meaning zigged when I thought it was about to zag and threw me off rather like a bucking bronco.

What am I saying, sir? Are you asking me what I am saying or what I am doing?

I was asking what you were saying, but now I want to know what you are doing! Like, for example, why do you have that long, sharp-looking knife?

Why do I have this long, sharp-looking knife? Is that what you're asking me?

Yes! What are you doing with it?

Why would you ask me what I'm doing with it when I'm simply doing what I'm told to be doing?

Stay away!

I told them that I wished not to kill the stranger who would come a-begging, yet this is what I was told to do, insistently, and thus, it seems, by the light of Hades, that it must come to pass, do you see?

Move away from me! Stop it!

And thus, apparently, despite my most fervent wishes, I must do it!

Help!

I must do it!

Help me! Someone!

Despite my most fervent wishes!

Aaahhh! Help! Please!

I do apologize! I did not wish this!

Aaaahhhh...

Thus it has come to pass!

Wait...

What?

Wait...

What, sir?

Come closer...

I can't hear you through the blood, sir. Closer... please...

I can't understand you, sir. The gurgling. Closer...

What?

Thank... you...

Thank you?

For granting my wish.

THE WISH BY KEVIN WEST © 2021.

KEVIN WEST IS A LONG-TIME MARKETING WRITER BASED IN LOS ANGELES, HAVING FUN WRITING SOME SHORT STORIES.

I'M A MURDERER

BY B. JOHN GULLY

I had a dream I killed my coworker. I'm late for work because of it. I oversleep until I hear his truck horn through my window. He keeps honking while I gather my things. The more he honks, the more I think my dream could come true today.

I rush out wiping the sleep from my eyes and climb into the truck.

'Rise and shine, buddy,' he says.

He calls me "buddy" even though he knows my name. It reminds me of how someone might talk to a dog.

'You gotta buy yourself an alarm clock.'

'I have one,' I lie. 'It didn't go off.'

He doesn't respond, rather lifts a bulky vaporizer to his lips and sucks nicotine. It crackles and whooshes. Cloudy vapor with a burning mint smell follows his exhale. Storm clouds form in the sky above us.

He says, 'Hope you brought your swim-trunks.'

'D'you think we'll finish early?' I say. 'With the rain.'

'We'll finish when we finish, buddy. Don't be a girl.'

At work we take turns hauling heavy gear and yanking jagged machinery. A lot of times I forget what we're doing. I'm too tired.

My coworker glares sometimes, resenting how

much weaker I am than him. Once, he told me he didn't understand how a guy could be so scrawny. I watch the muscles of his back flex through his shirt. He asks if I have a disease.

I remember something about my dream. Maybe I've known it all along, but I'm afraid.

It's him. He's going to hurt me today, when it rains, if I don't do what my dream said.

He calls from the truck. 'Buddy, finish up!'

I yank a thin wire slightly the wrong way. I'm distracted. It whips and slits the inside of my hand. I wince and watch blood emerge when I open my palm.

I yank open my backpack, trying to ignore the stinging. I search for the only thing I've looked forward to today: lunch.

My palm screams louder. Reality sets in. It's the worst case imaginable. I sigh.

'What?' my coworker says.

'I . . . forgot my lunch.'

'Want a protein bar?'

I look at him. His eyes are as sincere as I've ever seen them. The protein bar is chalky and leaves a pit in my stomach, but it's delicious— seasoned by hunger.

'Thanks,' I say.

He's silent. His vaporizer crackles. On the last bite of my impromptu lunch, I feel brave.

'Last night I had a dream,' I say. 'That I killed you.'

He drives, staring forward.

' . . . What is this, a sleepover? Don't tell me about your dreams, buddy.'

I look down at my feet.

The last job of the day always feels the longest. I

follow my coworker across a field on the side of the road, carrying our gear. He carries more than me.

There's a crunch under my foot that makes me stumble and drop a piece of equipment.

I look back at what I stepped on: a bird, half-dead. It looks bloated. Its eyes are still moving. A lump pulses near its head, as if a heart is soon to be evacuated through its beak.

'Buddy! Come over here, buddy. Come and look at what you did.'

It's like he's shoving my face into a pool of piss on a carpet. I hate him for it.

'Buddy, it's broke now, look! How're we supposed to finish? You gonna sew it back together?'

'I don't know I —'

I hear the crackling. It's like his vaporizer, but he isn't smoking. Whooshing permeates my ears, surrounding me. I realize it's starting to drizzle.

I open my hand and look at the gash on my palm. It starts to open more. I can see the inside of my skin. It closes, and then opens again, the flesh flapping.

It's a mouth, talking to me, squeaking in a weak little voice.

It says, '**Crush the head!**'

A few droplets pour down my hand when it talks, like blood but darker— almost black.

'**Pull out his eyes and swallow them whole!**'

'Buddy,' he says. He's standing in front of me, his hulking body betrayed by a look of fear.

I hold out my hand so he can see my gash talk. It doesn't say anymore words, rather it moans in a high pitched coo, like a baby.

My coworker shivers like a petrified animal. Then he stops and looks at his own hand.

He says, 'My ... skin's ripping ... buddy— getting one like you.'

He shows me his hand as it opens. A gash is in the same place on his palm. It flaps open and says to him, '**Protein.**'

'I can see my bones moving,' he says.

He looks at me, waiting for a reply.

'I'm a murderer.'

I step forward and pick up the piece of equipment I dropped.

'Look what I did,' I say, showing him. He shivers again. His eyes are terrified, melancholy.

The gear is so heavy I struggle to lift it. My palm screams in pain while I do. If I try to throw it, it would land a foot in front of me.

My coworker sees me struggling. He stops shivering and steps forward to help.

Easily, he lifts it over his head, looks up, and lets it fall onto his face. It drives his head into the ground. The rest of his body drops. I hear his head crunching, crackling. His feet twitch. The air whooshes.

I look away, feeling tears come on. I don't know what's wrong with me ...

... I'm tired ...

... He drives me home with the crushed husk of his head's remains.

At my house he turns to me, eyelessly, and says, 'Seeya tomorrow, buddy.'

I'm tired. I go inside and go to sleep.

THE WORKDAY BY B. JOHN GULLY © 2021.

B. JOHN GULLY IS A LITERARY FICTION WRITER BASED IN BOSTON MA, WHO CURRENTLY WORKS IN MENTAL HEALTH AND HOUSING CRISIS INTERVENTION. HE HAS A MASTER'S IN PSYCHOLOGY WITH A SPECIALTY IN EXISTENTIAL PSYCHO-DYNAMIC THERAPY. SO FAR HE HAS PUBLISHED AND PROMOTED SHORT-WORKS VIA SOCIAL MEDIA @3GULLY. HIS MODEST, BUT LOYAL, READERSHIP HAS BEEN ACQUIRED ENTIRELY THROUGH SELF-PROMOTION. HIS IS CURRENTLY QUERYING LITERARY AGENTS TO REPRESENT HIS DEBUT NOVEL, A LITERARY COMING-OF-AGE STORY SET IN OXFORD.

THE TWELVE DAYS OF CHRISTMAS

BY DAVID MCVEY

'You! I'll no tell ye again about sleeping here. This is Government property! Come on! Move!'

The young policeman stood, hands on hips, just inside a half-demolished cellar with an entrance like a cave. Cha looked up at him, shook himself awake, and wondered why the man was so protective of this hole in the wall and the weed-grown, rubble-strewn half-acre that adjoined it.

The cellar was long, dark and narrow as a grave; the policeman had to step aside to let Cha out. He looked on with disgust as Cha left his bed - just dirty blankets and cardboard boxes - and then added, 'I'll be watching for ye, mind; don't bother trying to come back!'

Cha lived alone; he did not care for the crowded hangouts where many of the city's homeless gathered for the night. The others knew that Cha liked his own company, and stayed away; he liked it that way, and the others respected his privacy.

The day had dawned wet and raw under slate-grey December skies; Cha made for the city streets, safe in the knowledge that the evening policeman was more tolerant. The city centre was already thronging; Salvation Army bands were tuning up and buskers were playing to bumper audiences. More and more people poured off buses and trains and out of car parks, swelling the armies already battling from shop to shop. Christmas was just over a week away.

Cha wandered on, stopping here and there, sheltering from the rain in malls and railway stations until he was moved on. In early afternoon, gales of laughter erupted as office parties spilled out into the streets. The sea of people only parted when Cha passed through; mothers led away their children at the very sight of him. Cha wasn't dismayed. He didn't trouble with *feeling* any more. He just lived and moved and had his being.

Some time after one o'clock a break in the weather allowed him to reach the Mission Hall dry in time for the homeless people's Christmas lunch. As he entered, a firm hand grasped his; 'Hullo, there - Cha, isn't it? Come away in!' One of the Mission staff showed Cha to a seat; he sat down amongst the bellowing laughter and toothless chortling. He found himself enjoying the meal; it was a novelty to be waited on, like in a restaurant. When all of the guests had been served, the Mission staff sat down and joined them.

The tables were cleared, and the Mission Superintendent rose to speak; a few of the guests switched off and began bickering amongst themselves, but others, like Cha, listened attentively to the message of Christmas, to words of hope, rebirth, salvation.

Cha recalled his first twelve-day alcoholic oblivion; it had straddled the New Year, perhaps nine years ago now, he couldn't be sure. In the months that followed he lost his wife and family, was sacked from his job, and started drinking away his home.

The meeting broke up. Cha averted his eyes when

the Mission Superintendent shook his hand, and then moved back into the street. The majority of the crowd went off to celebrate in the only way they knew. Cha himself rarely drank now; that wasn't what kept him on the streets. He just lacked the ability to change.

He shambled back through the city centre, ignoring the taunts of a group of teenage boys. A Salvation Army band struck up *The Twelve Days of Christmas*. It was now late afternoon and Cha decided to return to the hole in the wall before the chill of evening stalked the streets. The Christmas lights were left behind and a charcoal sky strove to overpower the streetlamps. The sound of the music began to fade.

Cha could not get to the hole in the wall; the fence around the site had been repaired and a new notice on a large hoarding soared above it. It listed contractors and consultants and clients, and ended:-

JUNCTION 19 SLIP ROAD
Work commences January 6th

The distant band, still playing *The Twelve Days of Christmas*, could barely be heard, now.

THE TWELVE DAYS OF CHRISTMAS BY DAVID MCVEY © 2021.

DAVID MCVEY LECTURES IN COMMUNICATION AT NEW COLLEGE LANARKSHIRE. HE HAS PUBLISHED OVER 120 SHORT STORIES AND A GREAT DEAL OF NON-FICTION THAT FOCUSES ON HISTORY AND THE OUTDOORS. HE ENJOYS HILLWALKING, VISITING HISTORIC SITES, READING, WATCHING TELLY, AND SUPPORTING HIS HOME-TOWN FOOTBALL TEAM, KIRKINTILLOCH ROB ROY FC.

WHERE THE HAPPINESS GOES

BY PADDY MCKENNA

She steps back from the door onto the footpath and looks up to my bedroom window. I pull my head back in, as quickly as I can, and let the curtains fall shut. It was only a second, could she have spotted me? The bell rings again and Lily shouts up from the street.

'Dinny, I know yer in there. C'mon.'

I don't want to see anyone. Not today, especially. The phone screen tells me that it's after 1pm. They'll be up at the graveyard now so what's Lily doing outside the house in her black dress?

'It'll only be a minute. C'mon, it's starting to rain.'

Her voice echoes through the hallway and into my bedroom at the top of the stairs. She's talking through the letterbox. There's no way she'll just leave. I pick up a crumpled bomber jacket and throw it straight on with no t-shirt underneath. I can't remember how long I've had my sweatpants on. Days anyway. She won't care.

Stepping down the wooden staircase in my socks, I open the door. Lily is staring back up towards the top of the town. She spins around and gives me a crooked smile. Her hair is wet from the rain. But the shower is already finished and the sun is back out. Droplets on the shoulders of her black dress look like diamantes sparkling in the sunshine.

'Finally. Can I come in? Got drenched there.'

I nod and move back to give her room. Once indoors, she stands aside for me and I walk silently towards the kitchen.

'They're gone up to the graveyard,' she confirms, and then, pulling herself up a seat in the kitchen, 'I met yer dad at the church and he said that ya were here and that I should come up and see ya.'

I nod and flop into the busted armchair, drawing my knees up to my chest. Lily goes to fill the kettle from the tap at the sink.

'How ya feeling?'

She clicks the kettle on and turns back to look at me.

'Fine.'

I slip my hand down the side of the chair and locate something round and plastic stuck there. My fingers explore the contours, though I already know it's the screw cap of a milk carton. I pull it out and start to move it between the gaps of my knuckles like a coin.

'Well, ya look like hell,' she says, turning back to pour water into the cups, and then, with her back to me, 'and ya smell like Rat's laundry basket.'

She turns around to face me with a cheeky grin, but that disappears when she sees my face. I'd like to laugh, and she's the only person who I want to see right now, but I have a hollow in my chest where the happiness goes.

She's about to say something but stops, and then, tapping her forehead like a reset button, she starts again.

'Rat's asking after ya. Royar, too. Ya haven't been on Whatsapp for days now.'

She stays standing by the steaming kettle, a look of concern on her face that I haven't seen before. I turn the screw cap over and over between my thumb and middle finger.

'No.'

I look up in time to see her grimace.

'Lookit, everyone's worried about ya, Dinny. Yer Dad, too. We're all here for ya if ya want to talk about it.'

Lily's voice sounds far away and echoey, like she's at the top of a well and I'm stuck right at the bottom. When I look at her she's surrounded by circular clouds of grey smoke, like rings of Saturn, that get bigger every time she speaks. The clouds were there for the guards that interviewed me, too. Hour after hour spent asking me about *the incident*, over and over. The same questions... describe to us the incident, give us a timeline for the incident, who saw the incident, whose idea was it that led to the incident... more and more grey smoke filling the room.

In the end, they seemed relieved to conclude that it was an unfortunate accident or 'gadding about' as one of them put it. Later on, they were able to put another name on it. Cause of death: misadventure. No charges. There was nothing further to investigate.

'Thanks very much,' I say to Lily, leaning back into the seat and closing my eyes. Talking requires so much effort. All I want to do is sleep.

'Here.'

When I look up again she's standing over me with the Crunchie mug in her hand. I take it from her, wrapping both my hands around the scalding hot surface. She walks back around the table and sits opposite me. Where Dad normally sits. It's strange to see her there. She's in my world. Mine and Dad's world.

'This is my favourite mug,' I say, hoarsely, tipping the cup to my lips.

'I had a feeling yer Dad or Diane weren't the ones drinking out of that bucket.'

The tea slips down my throat, raw from crying, and spreads warmth all the way down to my belly.

'That feel better?' she says.

'I'm not feeling very good, Lily.'

'I know, I know,' she says, softly. She takes a sip of her tea and looks down at the top of the mug. Behind her the cuckoo clock tick-tocks. Dad has left the radio on low and voices whisper in the corner of the kitchen like ghosts trying to offer us advice that is always just out of earshot.

WHERE THE HAPPINESS GOES BY PADDY MCKENNA © 2021.

PADDY MCKENNA IS A JOURNALIST AND MEDIA PRODUCER WORKING IN DUBLIN, IRELAND WHERE HE LIVES WITH HIS WIFE, JOANNE, AND TWO KIDS, MICHAEL AND JULIETTE. HE IS A FIRST-TIME AUTHOR, CURRENTLY FINISHING UP HIS DEBUT NOVEL, WITH NO PREVIOUSLY PUBLISHED WORK.

SOMETHING'S GOING ON IN THE STAIRCASE

BY ESTHER GONZÁLEZ

Rumors are always welcome. For there is nothing more frightening and wonderful than the shock wave of a rumor. It begins its journey in the building's doorway, harmless and pious. As it slips down the stairs and stumbles upon the corridor that separates one apartment from another, it begins to spread like a virus. It grabs hold onto the slippery banister that trembles to the rhythm of our footsteps, one after the other.

The lady in 2R told the widow of the 1L. The embroiderer of the 3R heard it through the cracks. The bulb of the staircase had burnt out.

My father was standing in the living room when I got out of my bedroom. He looked at me confused, something's going on. My brother soon appeared. He glanced at both of us, gawking, in complete silence, waiting for mom to issue the desired statement.

We can't leave the house, she finally declared. We knew it was best to let her speak and nod when her stinging gaze fell on one of us.

What happened? My brother jerked.

Who do you think I am? A psychic? Without light on the stairs, we can't get out.

We only had to open the door to confirm the rumors. From the fourth floor we heard the disfigured voices of our neighbors. The words rumbled through the walls until they became an echo as we carefully peeked out so as not to overstep the limits of our home. It didn't occur to us to go into the darkness that seemed capable of swallowing us. We kept at a safe distance, just as our neighbor, the painter, and his son, when they opened the door and found all four of us, our four heads sticking out where the narrow staircase ended, assessing the situation.

The light is gone, said the painter, and in the background we heard his wife whispering something. Yes, Salu, everything is dark out here. My mother pulled me aside to get a better look at them and asked if they knew where Jacinto was. To which he replied that he hadn't seen him since last week.

My mother grumbled, fidgeted, clamored kitchens closed. And disappeared to her room.

While the rest of us went about our business my brother stood motionless by the door, already shut. His face contracted into a question mark and his fingers interlocked. Later that night, I remembered he had just started dating a mysterious long-legged girl; holds her hair in a tidy bow, cherry-colored lips.

I'm going to make coffee, I proposed and dragged him to the living room table.

How long do you think we'll be like this?, he asked restlessly and with exaggerated effort stirred his coffee.

The truth that as long as the confinement lasted I wouldn't have to face reality, once clung to my head like gum on the sole of a shoe. I preferred to stay home and read the books I had accumulated over the past two years and looked at me defeated. Instead, I said: I am sure that everything will be OK. It's not a big deal.

How can you say that, he replied, no one has dared to cross the staircase, not even the widow of the 1L?

The widow has enough already, I joked. But he was too distracted to send such a complex order to his brain.

The days ventured the same for everyone, whether we wanted to or not. We woke up to the noise. Those who didn't know each other that well, now passed around recipes and chess moves. With a rope we delivered the pinch of salt or the sack of rice. From his window the painter would play sweet tunes on the guitar to put the children to sleep at night and lively songs to motivate them during the day.

I read *East of Eden* and *The Golden Notebook*. From time to time my brother needed to vent, he would lie on my bed and observe the lights reflected on the ceiling. My father started to read the newspaper at night. The baker on our street would lend it to the widow, who would then pass it on to the next neighbor. My father, then, informed us about that reality that we were gradually forgetting.

General happiness faded after two weeks. And without happiness, we lost hope that everything would return to normal. As much as the embroiderer reminded us of the importance of staying positive, uneasiness finally succumbed.

One morning, my mother woke up stubborn. More than usual. I can't take it anymore! She walked down the hall and opened the door, I'm going out, I don't care! The neighbors' pleas echoed everywhere: Stop! Nobody knows what's out there! Others encouraged her: It's time to do something! Let her go!

But in the end, she only cried until there was nothing else to be sad about.

A farewell to arms and Lorrie Moore's stories kept me unfazed when my mother unleashed her anger. From my room I could feel her vibrations trying to pierce my sensitive shell, enticing me to step out into the hallway and give her a reason to blame me for the garbage bags piled on the staircase.

Summer come and gone, and everyone thought that our confinement was coming to an end. The Asturian electrician would return to the neighborhood and restore order. Despite this, in September we still had no news from that skinny man who had fixed our refrigerator months earlier. The widow kept us informed and ordered groceries when necessary. Every Friday we poked our heads out in the courtyard and tossed the letters we wanted her to deliver.

It was a pity mine's always slipped through the tiny crack in the staircase. God would've loved my writing; ruthless, so sentimentally detached.

PART 4

*'Your mother was another
story altogether.'*

A MIGRATION

BY LYDIA BENSON

SECOND PLACE WINNER

In the beginning it was just you and me. Perhaps just me, from my perspective. You were the extension that was warm and singing. You were black hair and green eyes.

At first, we were in the back room of the old Victorian house. You fed me in bed against the red wall, illuminated by the last of the evening sun. I was small, I was yours.

You carried me to school, held me to your chest zipped up in your jacket like a baby bird. We walked up the big hill and chattered to one another over buses and cars and the sounds of the city. You dropped me off and I became one of them, in amongst it all, until I could leave.

One day you gave me your cardigan to hold, to stop the tears. I smelt it for the rest of the journey. Soon after, it faded. You became a voice on the phone. You said you loved me infinity times a million. I sat on the stairs and tried to remember your smell.

You had gone there to set things up. Far far away. You were finding work and a house.

I was painting my nails glitter green and listening to techno with the au pair. Paloma. She shaved off her red curls and died the stubble blue. Paloma. Wild and young. She loved me and you weren't there, so I drank

162

it up. Paloma. We bathed together. She ran naked into the sea.

Later, I was colouring in with the welfare officer, answering questions. She sat me down, handed me the paper. Draw a line, she said, fill the page with it. Then we coloured it in. Whilst I was reaching for pencils, trying to keep within the lines, she made me a little informant. It was fed back.

Around that time, you came back to the city. To court. To answer questions. Then you won.

We were suddenly in the silence. In the moon and stars and lambs in the fields. There was space then. You gave me my own room and we made friends at the church. Squeaky clean friends who shared their sweets. They were the parallel universe us: Irish parents, still together. I was small and grubby, faulty somehow. Loosened stitches and misshapen on a forgotten corner of the toy-shelf. Alone in a dark wood, overlooking a ravine. The sweets made me sick.

Years passed. You worked all day and then the evenings. You lost your dad. You became quiet. Then withdrew. Piece by piece.

Your eyes were veiled with cataracts of thought.

Once a double-glazing salesman came over. You were his dream, vacant and looking for instant gratification. I sat with you on the threadbare sofa in the front room, cold in the blue light of winter, and listened to the pitch. He was right. He understood you. You did want us to be warm; you did want to spend less, eventually; you did want to do something that might help with the damp, the creeping black in the top corners of the rooms. He was bursting out of his buttons, eyeing me cautiously each time I said I wasn't sure you had to decide right now, laughing and joking that I was a little adult already. You signed the papers.

Darkness slipped in after that, more and more. You were barely there. You ploughed, unseeing, through pensioners in the street. They looked back at you disgusted or shocked, but you were somewhere else entirely and no-one could come with you. Panic fluttered around the edges of the house. I watched you in high alert, then sloped off to the woods to get high with the glow worms.

You went off sick.

It was a different kind of space then. The sun came back.

In the mornings, you were home in the kitchen drinking coffee, listening to the radio. Unfurling. You told me about your childhood and cycling your Hi Ho Silver. You cried about your dad.

We went to Barcelona, just you and me again. You got the dates wrong and I missed school, but we saw moonscapes and buses with standard lamps on, so it didn't matter. We walked everywhere and drew everything and you talked. And listened. A little window.

At eighteen, I left. You took me and we drove all the way with my life in the boot. I came back less and less, moved further away. When I remembered, I called you. From airports, from mountains, from ancient neon cities. Standing at phone booths, I touched number pads greasy from other fingers, and burnt under the sun of a different hemisphere as I filled you in. Sometimes you struggled to hear me over the racket of cicadas, or the fragments of strangers. I became the voice on the phone. And as time went on, I left bigger gaps in between.

Sometimes, at night, I think wild birds have been let loose in the house. Their heavy wings batter through the rooms until they rest messy in my rafters. I open the window to let in the air. The sky is indigo twilight. Flaming balls of orange ignite one by one. I see you. Small, white hair, green eyes. You look keenly around, taking everything in. You draw the sea. I'm glad you're here, I want to say.

A MIGRATION BY LYDIA BENSON © 2021.

LYDIA BENSON IS AN EMERGING WRITER AND ILLUSTRATOR, BROUGHT UP IN CORNWALL AND NOW BASED IN A SMALL, COASTAL TOWN IN THE SOUTH-EAST. SHE IS CURRENTLY WORKING ON HER FIRST NOVEL. THROUGH WRITING AND ILLUSTRATION, SHE EXPLORES MEMORY AND PLACE.

NO ONE'S DREAM

BY BENJAMIN BRITWORTH

I don't know why ＿＿ hit me.

＿＿ said it's 'because you cried.' I tried not to, but a million tears rolled down my cheeks. My eyes ached. My voice turned to ribbits, like a frog. Mum said nothing when it happened. She smoked rolled up fags and drunk from a bottle. It looked like water, but it wasn't. Mum hasn't ever hit me, but she never stopped ＿＿ hitting me. She laughed when ＿＿ did it that time. Her teeth showed. Some were black. One was chipped.

＿＿ hit her once. She cried, hugged me and said, 'We'll get through this, babe. Bad day, eh? Bad day.'

She put black gunk on her eyes. When she cried, the gunk mixed with her tears and they turned black too. Her face got squiggly lines down it and her eyes turned red. I didn't like it when she cried.

I don't like crying either. But most of all I don't like it when ＿＿ hit us.

Mum said ＿＿ looked after us. ＿＿ didn't. She didn't think so either. I know that. Once she said 'I'm just lying to me'self' and sighed. But she never broke up with ＿＿. I don't think she could.

＿＿ isn't my dad. My dad's grave is covered in brambles. Great big juicy blackberries grow there in the autumn. Mum and I pick them. Mum said Dad died before I was born. It had to be true.

One time ___ hit me really bad. Mum and I got home from school. ___ had drunk the stuff that looked like water. ___ smacked me with the bottle. I felt a crunch. My body went soft. Mum shouted 'No ___ , no!' That was the only time she shouted back.

I stayed face down on the floor. The back of my head felt wet. 'He's just a kid,' she said, 'He ain't done nothin.'

'He's no one,' ___ replied. 'Little piss ant. Ruining our lives.' Angels danced in my eyes.

Mum took me to the hospital. I got stitches. Four flat metal pins that stung. The nurse asked her how it happened. Mum said I fell.

The nurse tried to ask me, but Mum said, 'Don't be talking to my son. You got your answer.'

The nurse left. Mum was shaking. She put a hand on my shoulder, looked me in the eye and said, 'If any of them ask, tell them you fell. They'll take you away otherwise. You won't be able to see me again.'

Water filled my eyes. 'I don't want to leave you.'

'Then tell them you fell.'

Mum put me to bed. ___ wasn't home.

I looked up at the ceiling. The little angels had returned. One of them was sitting on the lamp. It put its finger to its lips. I fell asleep.

An hour later I was awake. My head hurt. Something shone under my bed. It was so bright I had to squint.

An angel fluttered into the gap. It came back a second later, beckoned me, and vanished again.

I pushed back my duvet and squatted on the floor. The light was dazzling. I couldn't see what was under there. I put a hand in front of my face and crawled under.

There were clouds. Gold dust glided around me. I felt small. Like I was no one.

I followed the angels. The ground fell away. I flew with them. Soaring higher than anyone has ever flown before. They carried me up and up. The gold formed trails around us, the clouds dispersed. We were in the wide blue sky. Endless white stretched below. Then there was dark. The angels led me on. We flew for what felt like forever. I closed my eyes and drifted to sleep.

When I woke up, the angels had gone. I couldn't see anything. I tried to move, but there was nothing to push against. I floated. Lost.

A man spoke in the dark. He said, 'My boy. My glorious son! I'll get im back.' Then there was nothing.

In the morning, Mum came to see how I was. She checked the back of my head and said it looked better.

___ wasn't home.

Mum made me breakfast. Boiled egg. She cut the toast how I like it: little soldiers. The soldiers reminded me of the angels. I didn't tell Mum about them. They were secret.

Mum said I could have the day off school. She didn't talk about ___. The squiggly lines were under her eyes.

I got up and went for a wee. In the toilet I was dizzy and fell over. Mum came to help. She cleaned up the mess and took me back to my room. When she went to the shops I looked under my bed. There was my missing fire truck, and lots of dust. But the glowing clouds weren't there. Neither were the angels. I could taste blackberries.

Mum came home. She put the shopping in the kitchen. She was crying. I asked her why. 'They found ___ dead down Shipyard Way.' Fat black rivers ran from her eyes. 'No one knew where ___was until now. They said ___ fell, and that he was drinking. I don't believe it. Not down there. Someone hurt ___.'

I didn't say anything. I felt glad. I also felt bad. I didn't want ___ to come back. But I didn't want ___ to be dead either.

Mum cried all night. She drunk the water stuff too. She watched TV and ate a bucket load of ice cream.

I tried comforting her, before returning to bed. One of the little angels appeared on the lamp, put a finger to its lips, and disappeared.

NO-ONE'S DREAM BY BENJAMIN BRITWORTH © 2021.

BENJAMIN BRITWORTH IS AN AWARD-WINNING WRITER, FILMMAKER AND DESIGNER WHOSE WORK HAS BEEN SHOWN IN LONDON AND EDINBURGH, AND BEEN PRODUCED FOR THE FOREIGN OFFICE & THE JISC. HIS SHORT STORIES HAVE BEEN SHORTLISTED AND LONGLISTED FOR COMPETITIONS, AND SEVERAL HAVE BEEN PUBLISHED IN ANTHOLOGIES. HIS SHORT FILMS HAVE BEEN SHOWN AT UK FESTIVALS. HE OBTAINED AN MA IN COMPARATIVE CULTURAL ANALYSIS FROM THE UNIVERSITY VAN AMSTERDAM IN 2016, SPECIALISING IN NARRATOLOGY AND THE STRUCTURES OF CHARACTER EXISTENCE THROUGH POSSIBLE WORLD THEORY. HE RETAINS A KEEN INTEREST FOR ALL THINGS ACADEMIC.

MOTHERS' RUIN

BY YVONNE CLARKE

You rinse the cups with a metal scourer. It's not her fault she can't see the tea stains. Or the tear stains. She is *visually impaired*: 'partially blind' is an outdated, derogatory phrase these days. Sight loss is probably going to be your ultimate fate, too. A cruel blow for an inveterate bookworm.

So here you are, a full-time carer.

For someone you don't like.

We fail to recognise our parents' failings until we acquire the objectivity of an adult. You can love a parent without liking them. You loved your father and – yes – liked him too, the sort of like which would have made him one of your best friends if he had been your age.

Your mother was another story altogether.

'Don't get old, it's no fun: just give me a pill.' Your mother's melodramatic daily mantra.

'We're all on a one-way conveyor belt, Mum,' you reply. She stiffened, as she always did when you used to throw your arms around her as a kid. You don't remember her ever telling you she loved you. She wasn't that sort of person. Stiff upper lip, all that jazz.

'What have you done to the TV - it won't turn on?'

Her accusation cuts more sharply than any bread-knife. She was pressing the wrong button on the remote, as usual. To save time, you also select her favourite channel.

'What did you do that for? I'm not stupid.'

She sounds like a bluebottle banging itself against a window in frustration. You plan a temporary escape while *Dickie's Deal* is on TV.

'Fancy a cup of tea before I go cycling, Mum?'

'No, you know what my bladder's like. Why are you going out? You just leave me here like I don't exist.'

You execute a tiny shift in power play. 'I'm going out, Mum. I'll leave you a glass of water.'

You sense her invisible finger jabbing at you - stab, stab, stab - and her caustic words cause tears to prick your eyes like needles. Her way of instilling guilt is well practised.

◆ ◆ ◆

'About time. I'm dying for a drink.'

'I gave you a glass of water before I left. Fancy a cup of tea?'

'Need you ask? Not that disgusting Earl Grey you drink – it tastes like perfume.'

'I'm heating some soup for our lunch too.'

'Soup, soup, soup, that's all I ever have.'

'You don't like anything else, Mum.'

You bite the inside of your lower lip, hard. No wonder you suffer from bruxism. Retreating to the kitchen, you grab the novel you are halfway through. Is it worth ploughing to the end of this uninspiring choice from your book club, or should you move onto another paperback from the pile on the bookshelf? You decide you don't have the energy to tackle a new topic, new plot, new characters. Maybe tomorrow. You'll have a quiet ten minutes while the soup heats.

◆ ◆ ◆

The granny annexe took three months to build, and it took your mother less than three minutes to knock it down, metaphorically speaking. She's always had unrealistic expectations. And a sadistic streak, like a cat playing with a mouse. That nauseous feeling in the pit of your stomach begins to build again. How much longer can you expend mental and physical energy on satisfying your mother's demands?

◆ ◆ ◆

Don't take what she says personally, your counsellor advises. Many old people like to expend their diminishing control on creating chaos; rubbing people up the wrong way in the hope of getting a reaction. But the truth is that your mother's behaviour can't be blamed simply on old age. Her vindictive nature has always been directed towards you, and only you. Your patience is bursting like bubble wrap in your brain.

◆ ◆ ◆

'Would you like to go for a ride out today, Mum?'

'I want to see my solicitor. Change my will.' Her words are clipped, her mouthed tight-lipped.

Her veiled threat doesn't work. She's tried it before.

You look at this shell of a woman, your mother, and are overwhelmed by profound sadness. The age spots on her hands are merging into one mass of brown pigmentation. The jut of her jaw resembles that of a rabid dog. The curtains of closure have begun to surround her, like a coffin in a crematorium.

You're meeting Angela for a coffee soon. Angela's mother's in her nineties, too.

'Who's Angela?'

'Someone I used to work with.'

'Well, tell her you have a visitor.'

'But you're not a visitor, Mum; this is where you live now.'

'I might as well live on my own.'

For the sake of sanity, you need a gin and tonic, not a coffee. Angela would probably benefit from a G and T too.

'I love you, Mum, see you later,' you say, kissing the top of her head lightly.

You set off, tucking the bottle of Gordon's finest into your handbag.

MOTHERS' RUIN BY YVONNE CLARKE © 2021.

YVONNE CLARKE WORKED AS A COPY EDITOR AND CONTENT EDITOR FOR SEVERAL EDUCATIONAL AND BUSINESS PUBLISHERS BEFORE BECOMING A TEACHER OF ESL IN THE UK AND ABROAD. SINCE 2019 SHE HAS BEEN DEVOTING MUCH OF HER TIME TO WRITING FLASH FICTION AND HAS BEEN A RUNNER UP OR SHORTLISTED FOR A NUMBER OF COMPETITIONS.

CONNIE

BY LINDA MORSE

Go away. Not today. Fly, fly, bye-bye. Buy time, my time, time place.

My space.

See the floor grow into the walls. Crawl up the walls. Bright, sight, sun light through coloured glass. Turquoise, kingfisher blue. Fine shine, taffeta silk sheen on the walls. Gleam on the walls.

They don't know there's a mouse. Comes to chat, look at that no cat, when it's quiet... Someone drops crumbs on my bed. House mouse knows. Whiskers them away. Nibbles. Nibbles. Pretty pink hands.

'Here we are, Con. Nice cup of tea.'

Don't call me Con.

And it's not a cup, give up, upper cup, upper cut. It's a beaker leaker. Thing you give to babies. Don't think I'll drink. Not going to sink to that.

'Here we are.'

Clear, we are here. Too near. I wish you weren't. Interrupts my flow.

Go.

No, the silly woman comes in with her 'Here we are's' and Nice cups of tea'. Can't she see, I'm busy... organising my party.

'See you later, Con.'

You might. You might not. I might go out. Go out like a light. Give you a fright...

That'll thwart you, caught you, taught you, teach you teacher, preacher and your beaker leaker.

Don't like this blanket. Smells of mould and cold. I'm old. They told me, I'm old. Held a 'do'. How d'you do? Hullabaloo. My space was full of bodies. No idea who they were. Who's there? Don't care. Want some peace. 'This is your niece' Bluebell, Tinkerbell, Mirabelle, Daisybelle, or some dingling, dangling, jingling, jangle-spangled old person come on the day, all the way from New Zealand... or Wales.

A hundred. Telegram and foolish man... kept repeating, 'Century not out', 'Century not out'. Something about... football anyway. Any way at all.

He wasn't tall.

Door creak, smell leak, piss reek. And here she comes. Why do you enter my place in the world of my own making a noise?

'Time to take your tablets, Con.'

No.

Didn't take 'em yesterday, pesterday or the day before the war. Don't pretend anymore. Won't wait anymore to spit 'em out till after she's gone.

There. Learn who's who. What will you do? Who's boss? She's cross and I don't care a toss of the head of the bed.

'Come on Con, don't be difficult.'

Shit Spit Flit. It's gone. She's gone. Don't call me Con.

Face in the rug, smug rug – beady, black eyes and a long nose. Mother called it 'aquiline.' Very fine. She tried to better herself.

Ah! Here come *my* guests, not pest guests. Interesting people. Come by invitation, conversation, witty, pretty, ditty people. No tablets and beaker leakers. Respect me, directly address me correctly as Constance or Mrs. Brown.

Hello. Welcome.

Thank you. Yes I love this skirt. I bought it last week. New. Turquoise, kingfisher blue. Fine shine, taffeta silk sheen. Be seen. Be Queen of the night. Bright in the light, glittering sight, sweet delight.

Frank. So glad you could come. The party wouldn't be the same.

The dancing will start soon and swoon and over the moon.

Let's stand a moment together forever watching the rest in the glow and the flow and the show.

Look at his whiskers. And such beady eyes, aquiline nose, smart clothes and his spouse mouse has pretty pink hands?

Help yourself to crumbs. Nibbles. Nibbles.

Ah, the music's playing, swaying. First dance, first glance, last chance.

My oldest friend … in our timeless place. Handsome face. Grace and lace.

Last dance, last glance, last chance.

You've worn me out… but you haven't lost your touch. Such touch, so much touching, moving… moving away.

Ruby, I'm so glad you came. Yes, it's sad. Nothing lasts forever and a day.

Be nice to stay, but we're leaving as soon as the

party's over… to live in clover… nearly over…

Must you all go so soon… we've just begun… in the sun. It's set and there's hardly a moon… so soon… over so soon…

LINDA MORSE IS A DORSET WRITER AND PLAYWRIGHT, PART OF BOB (BEST OF BOTH) THEATRE. IN 2019, SHE TOURED A ONE-WOMAN SHOW ABOUT ADOPTION, 'A SHARED BREATH' AND THIS HAS NOW BEEN RECORDED AS A PODCAST. FOUR OF HER OTHER FULL-LENGTH PLAYS HAVE REACHED THE SHORT OR LONG LISTS OF THE TRAVERSE THEATRE EDINBURGH, BRISTOL OLD VIC OPEN SESSION, THE BLUE ELEPHANT THEATRE, LONDON AND / OR SALISBURY PLAYHOUSE NEW WRITERS AWARD. SHE HAS HAD SHORT PLAYS AND MONO-LOGUES PERFORMED IN LONDON AND THE SOUTH WEST. DURING 2020, WHEN THEATRE PERFORMANCE WAS IMPOSSIBLE SHE WAS INVOLVED IN CREATING A NUMBER OF SHORT FILMS AND VIDEOS AND BEGAN TO DEVELOP HER WRITING FOR RADIO / PODCASTS.

LET'S PRETEND

BY FRANCES GAPPER

As a child you often played Let's Pretend. Let's pretend I'm an orphan, let's pretend I'm an angel. All good practice for this new game: Let's pretend Mum's not dead.

You sit beside her on the sofa and hold her wrinkly freckled hand, patting it from time to time. Her bakelite clock ticks on the mantelpiece and silver foil squares protect the Indian Palace carpet from the mahogany furniture. She was a good mother to you, and still is. You decide to leave her gold wedding ring on. Even though Dad's long gone and it's worth a bit.

'Come on then, Mum.'

The air's left her bones and she's uncooperative. However it's just the night for a private burial. Next door's eucalyptus whispers and rattles. Mum hates that tree, it sucks her flower beds dry. The shrouded moon guides you along the path to her eternal bed, which is well rotted down apart from eggshells. Having sat her against the fence you poke away at it with Dad's trowel until it's thoroughly eviscerated. You lay her tenderly to rest. Vowing you'll often scatter the heap with peelings of her staple Fairtrade bananas and Gala apples, plus grapefruit segments for digestion.

She likes a hot water bottle, so nipping to the kitchen you fill her favourite red ribbed one and scoot back down to tuck it in.

Checking on her from your bedroom window, you say night night Mum. Sweet dreams.

Lovely to have her so close. It's a long bus ride to the cemetery.

If the council find out she's dead they'll terminate her tenancy and evict you. What then? A squeaky shopping trolley crammed with stuff you have to push ever onwards. Feet swaddled in rags and plastic bags. Wind shrieking through a dank underpass. Cold paving stones and bits of cardboard. Men pissing on you or setting you alight with petrol.

No. That's not going to happen.

People wave to you in the street. 'How's your mum?'

'Fine, thanks.'

LET'S PRETEND BY FRANCES GAPPER © 2021.

FRANCES GAPPER HAS PUBLISHED THREE COLLECTIONS OF SHORT AND SHORT-SHORT STORIES. HER WORK CAN BE SEEN ONLINE IN PLACES INCLUDING WIGLEAF, THE ILANOT REVIEW, THE CITRON REVIEW, NEW FLASH FICTION REVIEW, SPLONK AND SPELK.

BURNING LOVE

BY MARIE DAY

Mother's a stranger. But she crochets a doll every year for my birthday. I hold it close to my heart; name her Anna like my mother.

Grandma sets an extra place at the table for Anna. Between bites of lemon cake, we sing *Happy Birthday* twelve times for each year of my life. The three of us swing between rooms. Legs kick high on each beat, as though Teddy Foster and his band are there, playing in my grandparents' home.

Birthday parties are not for Grandfather. Not mine anyway. He scorches the celebrations, throws Anna into the fire.

Her eyes burn last.

'You could've let the child have the doll, William.' Grandma holds me back from the flames, smoothes hair from my tear-streaked face.

'Let's spare her from keepsakes that will bring embarrassment for years to come.' Grandfather leaves us with the charred pieces of my mother's love.

I cling to Grandma, bury my head in round shoulders. 'I didn't keep her safe. Will she still love me?'

'A mother's love burns in her heart forever, Ellen.' Grandma dabs the apron against her eyes. 'You're very much like her. Grandfather sees that.'

Late evening, and the scent of lavender soap follows

my grandfather around the house. Excitement flashes in his eyes; a night with friends at Milsons Gentlemen's Club ahead. She's singing there tonight. The woman in the photograph, Grandma calls a poor man's Jean Harlow.

Grandma knits tight her lips, sweeps soot from the hearth. Anger fills me. I stand in their bedroom doorway. Grandfather's lips twitch under the thick moustache as he bends to kiss Jean's photograph. 'Go to bed, Ellen.' He doesn't look my way, perhaps scared he'll see Mother in my face.

Grandma says it's the smile and waves of auburn hair. But not the eyes.

He needn't worry. I've no cause to smile yet.

By dusk, Grandfather sets off to outrun memories, chase brandy and a blond burlesque dancer.

He slams the door; relief creaks through the house. I edge towards Jean's photograph, take a long, wooden stick from the box. The strike and fizz of the match devour the silence. Fear dances in her eyes, the flame above, threatening. I press the match tip against the top corner. Watch the fire bite the paper.

Does this make me feeble-minded? That's what he says of Mother. His only daughter, sent to the asylum days after my birth, three years older than I am now. How we've heard of the suffering, forced upon Grandfather these past twelve years. Two families ripped apart. Painful accusations. The good name torn from that older, respected gentleman. A true friend. Like family.

Grandma says she doesn't understand. Will never understand. He can't bear Mother's smile on my face. Yet he looks into my eyes, over warm brandy glasses, every time he meets his friend at Milsons.

Jean surrenders to the flames so easily. How this will add to Grandfather's suffering.

I smile; the eyes burn last.

BURNING LOVE BY MARIE DAY © 2021.

MARIE DAY IS A WRITER, PART-TIME PRIMARY TEACHER AND FULL-TIME DAYDREAMER. ORIGINALLY FROM YORKSHIRE, SHE NOW LIVES NEAR BRISTOL WITH HER FAMILY. HER FLASH FICTION STORIES HAVE BEEN PUBLISHED BY NATIONAL FLASH FICTION DAY, @FLASH500 AND @MORESTORGY. SHE'S HAD ARTICLES AND CHILDREN'S STORIES PUBLISHED BY BBC ONLINE, WRITEMENTOR MAGAZINE AND AQUILA. MARIE IS CURRENTLY LOOKING FOR AGENT REPRESENTATION FOR HER MIDDLE-GRADE MAGICAL REALISM NOVEL. FIND HER ON TWITTER @MARIEDAYWRITING.

THE MAGICAL WHITE CANVAS SHOES

BY GAYATHIRI DHEVI APPATHURAI

COMPETITION FINALIST

I ask Giri what he learnt in school today. For a six-year-old, he learns things I can't even begin to comprehend. I wait for his animated anecdotes, but he opens and shuts his mouth a few times like a fish, no words coming out. He is itching to ask me something, but I don't prod further. I don't know what his question is, but I know that I don't have a convincing answer. More often than not, it is money.

I stack up some cotton sarees on top of a woolen blanket, as the floor is perpetually damp with the water leaking from the roof. Giri sleeps almost instantly, while I lay awake listening to the clinks of rainwater collecting in the vessel. The muted sound tells me it is full. I quickly pour out the water and put it back in place. I need to buy the blue tarp sheet for the roof, at least this monsoon.

As I am about to drift off, I hear faint murmurs. Giri shifts closer to me with eyes half-closed. 'My PT Teacher wants me to wear white canvas shoes for the running competition next week.'

❖ ❖ ❖

Giri is the designated runner boy of our lane; he does neighborhood deliveries for the tailor aunty down the street. He makes cheeky scooter sounds and zips through the lanes in a flash. Some of the old ladies feign annoyance at him racing up and down, but they love him dearly.

I carry his old slippers to the footwear shop, hoping to find something within my budget. The shopkeepers don't allow kids like Giri to try them on; they worry the shoes might get soiled. People without money, like us, take whatever life decides we are worth getting, nothing more. Giri has some more years to go before he fully understands this. I find a pair of white shoes that seems his size and ask how much they cost. The shopkeeper says seven hundred rupees. I quietly return them without a second glance.

Giri tells me how the other kids are training with running coaches, but he learns by simply observing them. I smile at his audacity. When he starts demonstrating some stretches he saw today, I catch him from behind and start tickling him. He rolls on the floor, laughing.

I see his unbridled excitement and make a silent promise to him that he will run in the competition.

◆ ◆ ◆

I ask for Madam's permission to leave early, so I could search in the local market for cheap shoes. I quickly wash the vessels and sweep the floor. As I dust out the cupboards, my eyes land on a pair of blue shoes, smaller than the rest. My glance lingers on them a moment longer, wondering if I can ever afford to buy such good shoes for Giri.

Madam summons me as I leave. She hands over a small plastic bag with her son's shoes, the blue shoes I saw earlier. She says they don't fit her son anymore; asks me to take it for Giri. I recoil in embarrassment; could my desperation be more obvious? But I keep my feelings buried, accept the shoes, and thank her for her generosity.

I come home preoccupied. Giri is doing an animated enactment of his running rehearsal to my engrossed neighbor, with dramatic sounds for added effects. The kid resolutely tells him that he will win first place.

I look at the blue shoes in my bag. I will find a way to turn them white.

◆ ◆ ◆

'Soak them in bleach,' my neighbor tells me. But I am wary of spoiling them. So, I carefully dab bleach on them. I notice some color fading off. After an hour, the shoes look pale, but still blue.

The tailor aunty takes the shoes from me and inspects them. She says they are big for Giri. She goes inside and starts rummaging through the piles of cloth bits next to her sewing machine. She comes back with some items and offers to stitch soft paddings to put inside the shoe. She says 'why don't you paint on the shoes? No one will notice from a distance. There is a special fabric paint for that.'

Giri doesn't breach the subject of shoes, but I can see he is getting restless. The kid is perceptive enough not to pressure me. I hope I can live up to my end of the promise.

◆ ◆ ◆

I couldn't find white fabric paint in any shop in the neighborhood. I need to make it work tonight, so I buy the usual white paint. I don't even know how good it will be.

Giri begs me to let him see the shoes, but I somehow convince him to wait until tomorrow. After putting him to sleep, I paint on the shoes with the white color until I finish the whole bottle. I leave them to dry in a safer place inside the house and hope they look good tomorrow.

I wake up to a yelp. Giri has already worn his 'white' shoes and jumps in joy!

◆ ◆ ◆

Giri stands fourth in the lineup of kids on the track. He waves at me and raises his thumbs, inviting some chuckles around me. The race begins; I see him lead, I see him trail, but never distracted. He simply runs because he loves to. He even does a little victory dance after finishing third in the race!

He proudly wears his medal the whole way back. A bout of rain comes unannounced, we scurry to the nearby bus stop for shelter. A few moments later, Giri shakes me hard and squeals.

'Ma, see, my shoes are magical! They have changed to blue color!'

I cry and laugh at the same time. I feel overwhelmed; at his happy mind that sees only light, at his un-tainted heart that has only hope.

'Yes, Giri, they are! The shoes are indeed magical.'

GAYATHIRI DHEVI APPATHURAI HAS AN ENGINEERING DEGREE
IN ELECTRONICS & INSTRUMENTATION AND WORKS IN THE
INFORMATION TECHNOLOGY INDUSTRY. HER SHORT STORY
HAS BEEN SHORTLISTED IN BRISTOL SHORT STORY PRIZE 2021
AND PUBLISHED IN THEIR ANTHOLOGY. SHE IS A TRAINED
INDIAN CLASSICAL CARNATIC VOCALIST AND HAS PERFORMED
IN RENOWNED FINE ARTS VENUES IN SOUTHERN INDIA. HER
OTHER CREATIVE PURSUITS INCLUDE PAINTING AND SCULPTING.
SHE LIVES WITH HER HUSBAND IN MUMBAI, INDIA.

LET'S PRETEND...

BY E.E RHODES

There's a rack of snappy postcards to choose from.
Let's pretend I picked one up and wrote it straight
away. Slotted it into the post-box. That I even had
a stamp and a pen in my handbag. That I was sufficiently on top of things to let you know I was okay.
Let's pretend...

The car had petrol. Let's pretend I remembered to fill
her up and had enough money from his wallet. Made
it to the garage. That I flirted with the attendant just
enough that she was shyly sweet back. That I wasn't
so scared or bright-bruised I frightened her. Let's
pretend...

The bag was packed. Let's pretend I was prepared,
and I'd thought about everything I needed. Had it
ready by the door. That I'd hidden it well enough he
wouldn't find it. That I was sufficiently pushed, I
finally grabbed my keys and left. Let's pretend...

The day was quiet. Let's pretend he'd gone to work
and somehow didn't double lock the door. No need
for lockpicks or the crowbar I'd sneaked into the attic.
That I waited long enough after he'd left. That I was
smart and patient and not too cowed to think. Let's
pretend...

The morning was bright. Let's pretend I slept
through, undrugged and not groggy from the pre-
scription the chemist reluctantly filled. Trying to

meet my eye. That he was kind but I wasn't ready. That I knew there were strangers who recognised all the signs I was trying to ignore. Let's pretend…

The booze was still in the bottle. Let's pretend I wasn't wrecked from drinking, just to make sure he'd not lose his rag. Doing all the right things so utterly carefully. That he'd have no reason. That he needed a good reason, not simply any reason at all. Let's pretend…

There was food on the table when he got home. Let's pretend I wasn't late back from work when the bus didn't come. The fridge was full. That we'd paid the electric too, so there was no excuse for it. That it hadn't all been spiralling for some not inconsiderable while. Let's pretend…

The people at work didn't bitch about me. Let's pretend I felt like there was someone I could talk to. Who'd simply listen. That it meant I knew it wasn't all on me. That I wasn't just a face ripe for fists and bruises. Let's pretend…

I even had a job. Let's pretend that I'd found a place with nice people. An hourly wage that didn't make him fret. That there were tips as well. That I was careful and showed my payslips at home, and was still in the position to save something too. Let's pretend…

My friends still called. Let's pretend he hasn't cut me off from them. Taken away my phone. That no one checks my texts and calls. That there was anyone left who knew me, not as I am now, but how I used to be. Let's pretend…

He and I never met. Let's pretend I wasn't in the bar that night. Sipping cocktails through a long straw with my friends. That I never smiled at his jokes, flirting. That I was as smart as I thought I was. Smarter even. Smarter still. Let's pretend…

There was no row with Mum that time. Let's pretend she wasn't pissed-off with me, said I ought to find a place. That by default Dad thought so too. That I knew when to keep my big mouth shut, with no intention of repeating that pattern again. Let's pretend…

I got a place at college and found a way to get out. Let's pretend I lived up to the promise that Mrs Barnes the English teacher saw. Writing poetry and stories, even winning that prize. That I used my words wisely. That I took the application home and we all talked it over, Mum and Dad both getting excited too. Let's pretend…

There was no expulsion and I didn't screw up those opportunities. Let's pretend I wasn't a total fish out of water, wasn't even a frog who at least has a chance. That I couldn't hardly breathe in every class. That I had any clue what all the rules were, or even that there were any rules to know. Let's pretend…

Those exams were just fine. Let's pretend Mum let me study, even though it meant I didn't skivvy every day after school. That I only worked at my uncle's place on Saturdays, to help out with the bill brown envelopes. That we had enough to more than cover all the corners without endless hours of bickering. Let's pretend…

I didn't daydream my way through most classes. Let's pretend I dreamed in sunlight, not to get away from the night. That some things we don't talk about, ever. That every family has secrets, and some you know you don't lay out with the plates and cutlery on the kitchen table. Let's pretend…

I didn't try and tell Sister Mary-Thomas. Let's pretend she didn't slap my face and tell me I was awful. Terrible child. That she didn't tell my parents. That I wasn't always the one who must be lying, and I should be grateful for the family who loved me. Let's pretend…

My uncle never even looked at me. Let's pretend he wasn't Mum's favourite younger brother. That he wasn't so tall and big to me. That he didn't realise his power, and of course that I knew how to disappear for real, not like in my books where that was make-believe. Let's pretend…

I made it out of the hospital unbroken. Let's pretend I wasn't hit by that car. Stupid drunk driving. That everyone believes will never be them. That my childhood was utterly uneventful and loving. That I even made it beyond six years old unscathed to send happy postcards from anywhere at all. Let's pretend.

LET'S PRETEND BY E.E RHODES © 2021.

E. E. RHODES IS AN ARCHAEOLOGIST WHO ACCIDENTALLY LIVES IN A CASTLE IN ENGLAND, WITH HER EQUALLY SURPRISED PARTNER, MANY BOOKS AND PROBABLY LOTS OF MICE. SHE WRITES FLASH, CNF, AND SHORT PROSE POETRY TO MAKE SENSE OF IT ALL.

WHAT GOES AROUND

BY DAVID LEWIS

… so Glyn brought his intended to see me today I
assumed he'd put her in the family way he said no he
just loved Jean and they want to get married I said
congratulations Jean seems nice enough pretty smiling curly hair flowery frock said polite things about
my flat not sure she meant them anyway it's clear
we're not the same kind and oh god is the same thing
happening all over again I've done my best by Glyn
since Dick died dear Dick I never should have gone
with because he brought shame on my family and his
family they thought they were a cut above me being
the eldest of 13 and going into service at 12 not that I
minded really it got me a room of my own and away
from helping Mam with the six others that were there
more to come and then I worked as a skivvy for five
shillings a week plus board and lodging years and
years on my knees making up fires before the family
got up peeling potatoes ironing long-johns and panta-
loons till they made me cook and going to Chapel in
Pontypridd every Sunday and promising not to drink
or have anything to do with men until I was married
but how do you meet a man to marry if you don't have
anything to do with them and when I was 25 there

was a fair at the farm with a maypole and Dick was
there hardly any hairs on his chin seven years younger
skinny still at school but he had a nice smile and asked
me to dance I knew I shouldn't the Minister warned
against dancing but Dick gave me cider he said was
apple juice the Chapel warns against the demon drink
and he swung me around till I needed to lie down Dick
took me into the hayloft where he undid his trousers
and asked me to touch his giblets and take off my
knickers and then you can guess what happened it
didn't last long thank God it was messy and I didn't
like it but Dick said we were like Shakespeare and Ann
Hathaway all I knew about Shakespeare was he wrote
Romeo and Juliet I thought that was nice but Dick said
I was more like Ann because she was older and they
had it off on Midsummer too which made me feel
better but then Dick said Ann got a bun in the oven
and her family made him marry her and it was like
that with me about the bun in the oven I mean but his
parents were against us getting married Dick was
their only one their pride and joy he was lined up for
university they wanted the baby adopted but Dick
stuck by me which showed he was a good man the
family where I'd been for 13 years said they didn't
want a tart like me in their house so I had nowhere to
go mam didn't want me back I was a bad example to
my brothers and sisters and Dick's family wouldn't
take me in so Dick had to leave school and go to the
mines to earn money for a room thank goodness he
got a job above ground he wasn't strong I would have
worried sick if he'd had to go down the pit when the
mine closed we moved to Croydon and never saw his
family again they never forgave Dick or me for dragging Dick down but we've shown them now because
Glyn is far better than any of them he won scholar-
ships to the grammar and university which is more

than any of them can say and now he's met this
woman Jean at his college nice enough pretty studies
English like Dick wanted to she's C of E but willing to
become a Methodist for Glyn but what will her family
say about her marrying someone whose ma's a dinner-
lady and rents a council flat it's marrying down like
Dick marrying me she says her father's chief clerk in a
bank and they have a house with a name not a number
and a maid like I was years ago I couldn't help being a
skivvy how could I help being born into a poor home
with mam having children year after year till she went
through the change she couldn't keep Dad off her the
last one's called Gladys she's younger than Glyn
though she's his aunt Glyn is good to me but I know
he's ashamed because he kept me away from his school
didn't want the teachers and parents to meet me and
perhaps he doesn't really want me to meet Jean's
parents and it's Jean that insists I'm ashamed because
they won't want their daughter marrying down
they'll be embarrassed and I won't know what to wear
or what to say or how to say it not that I'm any worse
than they are but I haven't had their advantages the
Minister said I had beautiful handwriting and it's a
shame I couldn't stay at school I'm not sorry I brought
Glyn into this world and didn't give him away he's a
good son but I made sure I never had another I told
Dick he mustn't come near me again after the hayloft
even after our wedding his family refused to attend
and then Glyn arrived we told everyone he was very
premature because it was less than six months after
we got married no-one believed us of course because
Glyn was a normal size and then Dick died when Glyn
was five and I never slept next to another man didn't
want one though my lodger Tom tried it on and even
asked me to marry him I said no of course but now I
wonder if I was right now Glyn's brought his intended

194

to meet me and …

WHAT GOES AROUND BY DAVID LEWIS © 2021.

DAVID LEWIS HAS WORKED AS A FOREIGN CORRESPONDENT,
WRITER ON AIDS FOR WHO, AND SPOKESMAN FOR THE EUROPEAN
BROADCASTING UNION. HE NOW LIVES AND WRITES IN FERNEY-
VOLTAIRE, NEAR FRANCE'S BORDER WITH SWITZERLAND. HIS EARLY
COLLECTION OF SONNETS WON A PRIZE AT CAMBRIDGE UNIVERSITY.
SEVERAL STAGE PIECES HAVE BEEN PREMIÈRED IN GENEVA AND
PUBLISHED IN THE ANNUAL LITERARY REVIEW EX TEMPORE.
THE FIRST CHAPTERS OF HIS THIRD NOVEL, MADE IN HUNGARY,
WERE PUBLISHED BY PANORAMA JOURNAL AND NOMINATED
FOR A PUSHCART PRIZE. HE HAS BECOME A KEEN FLASHER SINCE
JOINING THE RETREAT WEST COMMUNITY. IN 2021 HE WON
THE BANGOR 40 WORDS COMPETITION FOR MICRO-FICTION.

PROFIT AND LOSS

BY KEVIN CHEESEMAN

The sun was barely up when Grant unlocked the shop, but already he was thinking about the grief he'd have to face when he got home. Karen resented him leaving the house so early and accused him of running away. He'd argue that it was to catch guys going out for a day's sport in the countryside: they'd come in for bait or cartridges, and he'd persuade them to buy some new gear. Trouble was, the customers weren't convinced, and Karen wasn't buying it either. And to-night, when her parents came over for dinner, he'd get it in the neck from them too.

Grant flipped the sign on the door to 'Open' and headed to his office at the back.

He could pretty much predict how the conversation with Karen's parents would go. George would ask how Grant's 'little shop' was doing and offer again to look over his business plan. He'd enquire, in his offhand way, about when Grant 'might be in a position' to repay their loan. And Christine, half as subtle and ten times as sanctimonious, would go on again about how 'uncomfortable' they were with Grant selling firearms.

Didn't they get it? If he went back to only selling

fishing tackle, they'd never get their damn money back.

He put some coffee on to brew and tried to clear his head by contemplating Megan's inexpert drawing of 'Daddy's Shop', on the wall by his desk. Even today, the 'Rods and Rifels' sign made him smile.

The shop door opened, and a familiar voice called his name.

'In the back, Nick,' he replied.

Nick, clad head-to-toe in camouflage gear, seemed to fill the small office.

'How's it going, Grant?'

'Never better. How about you? Is it ammo you're after?'

'You bet. There's a big old boar out there with my name on his back.'

'Isn't it time you retired that old Remington? You should treat yourself to a new gun in time for the deer season.'

'Oh, please, not that again.'

'Just take a look at this,' said Grant, undeterred. He unlocked a cabinet and took out a hunting rifle. Its long barrel, a lustrous bluish-grey, emerged from a smooth, exquisitely sculpted walnut stock.

'I got this in for a guide down in Rockbridge. Try it.'

Nick raised the rifle and took aim at an imaginary target.

'Feel that balance?' said Grant. 'Easy action. High-precision. Softer kick than a baby.'

Nick weighed it in his hands.

'It's a beauty, all right.'

He handed it back.

'But I don't make the kind of money those guides do.'

Grant nodded.

'Maybe next season, huh?'

As Grant replaced the rifle, Nick pointed at another gun in the cabinet.

'Woah – is that an AK-47?'

'Sure is. Well, a Chinese copy.'

Grant unfolded the stock, clipped in a magazine, and passed the gun over.

Nick held it awkwardly in front of him.

'No way this is for hunting.'

'It's for a collector down in Martinsville. I already sold him two, now he wants another. Who am I to argue?'

'Huh. Ugly brute, if you ask me. Damn ugly. Anyway, how about that ammo? I need to get going.'

When Nick had gone, Grant dismantled the Kalashnikov, ready for delivery. Nick was wrong, he thought. Sure, it lacked the sleek lines of the hunting rifle, but it had a certain style about it.

After he'd finished parcelling it, he was unsure what to do. The last thing he'd said to Karen was that he was going to deliver the gun in person, a three-hour drive to Martinsville. She'd made it pretty clear what she thought of that idea.

'You win,' he sighed. He labelled the package with a black felt-tip pen, sent an email to say it was ready for collection, then sat down to deal with the online orders.

The morning ticked by, bringing a trickle of customers wanting the usual small stuff: bait, hooks, cartridges. Then – nothing. At three o'clock, bored and frustrated, Grant flipped the sign to 'Gone Fishing' – and went fishing.

He switched his phone off and brooded for hours by the sullen river, looking for answers in the murky water.

Customers like Nick, he decided, were a waste of time. They spent a few dollars here and there on bullets or bait and bought maybe one gun their whole life. There wasn't much profit in that. The only way he could get out from under was to double down on the online gun business and reach out to the collectors, the guys who spent big money on a repeat basis.

He'd talk it through with Karen. She was smart; she'd get it. And she'd support him like she used to do before her condescending parents started interfering.

Grant jumped into his pick-up and sped home, the CD player blasting out Karen's favourite song: 'Throw Your Arms Around Me'.

As he stepped through the front door, Karen caught him with a slap that knocked him sideways.

'Where the hell have you been?' she said. Then she pulled him close and sobbed into his chest. 'I thought you'd gone to Martinsville.'

'No. Why? Has something happened?'

'Haven't you heard? Some guy down there has gone crazy, shooting people.'

Karen's mother emerged from the living room, ushering a confused looking Megan in front of her.

'Let's get this little one to bed, Karen,' said Christine. She looked accusingly at Grant. 'She shouldn't see this.'

Grant joined George in front of the TV.

'It's awful, Grant. Horrific.'

Grant absorbed the news – fifteen people killed, the gunman holed up – and when he heard the shooter's name, he could picture it written on a package in black felt-tip.

His stomach lurched. The TV images – an isolated house, policemen crouched behind cars – seemed dreamlike. The newscaster's voice was muffled and distant.

'Fifteen people shot dead. Five of them children.'

'Grant?'

George was speaking to him.

'Grant – do we need to talk, son?'

PROFIT AND LOSS BY KEVIN CHEESEMAN © 2021.

KEVIN CHEESEMAN LIVES WITH HIS WIFE IN HADDENHAM, BUCKS, UK. HE HAS A PHD IN BIOCHEMISTRY AND HAS RECENTLY RETIRED AFTER A CAREER IN CLINICAL RESEARCH. KEVIN IS NOW EXPLORING CREATIVE WAYS TO SPEND HIS TIME, INCLUDING WRITING SHORT STORIES.

WHISKEY TO MILK

BY TRACEY-ANNE PLATER

Today is our fortieth wedding anniversary. You mesmerised me from the moment we met. You were older than me and alluringly subdued, with a car that smelt of cigars and soil, and a smile that made me blush. I tried everything to get your attention, and when it finally worked, I felt I'd won the most fantastic prize. I put you before my friends, family, career, dreams, self-respect.

It was an impossible goal, but I wanted you to love me more than you loved the poison. I changed my hair, my habits, my food. I danced to your music, watched your films, indulged in your addiction. Whiskey at 7 am and meaningless purchases to clutter our tobacco-stained flat.

We became parents; this helpless being that baffled us both so much made you smile. I'd done it! I'd finally made you happy. Bottles of milk replaced bottles of whiskey, and sleepless nights were with our baby and not the poison. The novelty eventually wore off, but the drink had kept its appeal and welcomed you back with virulent arms. You went headfirst into its trap, and I haven't seen you since. The real you – the one I glimpsed when I gave you our baby. The one that smiled at me while I lay numb in a hospital bed.

I've thought about leaving many times, escaping the sneers, putdowns and taunting. But now you're dying, which is so very much like you—always putting obstacles in the way of my happiness. They say you may only have a month left, and you want to spend it sat in that chair, refusing help and turning the same colour as our tobacco-ridden walls. I've packed my holdall several times. I even bought a train ticket once.

'Where's my whiskey? I asked you to get some more bloody whiskey! Are you useless?' you say, with the voice I have come to despise and those soulless mustard eyes.

You weren't like this at first. You were entertaining and merry. But I soon realised that wasn't real. Once the alcohol drained from your system, there were no smiles or affection. Do you know we have never held hands while you have been sober? I lost count of the times I cried in our bed after another snub from the resentment that was your brief sobriety. You dismantled my heart over the years – piece by piece. The birthday you told me you couldn't afford a gift for, only for me to find you wobbling around town with your new paisley shirt and the dark aroma of malt. The engagement party that you let me arrange, but you didn't turn up to. Your boss's daughter who called the home phone the morning after the work Christmas party.

You noticed when my waistband became tight but never complimented an outfit. Sometimes I just wished you would tell the truth – that you never wanted me. Not really. I happened to you, and you made your drunken peace with it. By the time you sobered up, it was too late to tell me I was a mistake.

You bought flowers for women that should surely be less important to you than I. You laughed when I said I wanted to join the police. I watched you throw my childhood diaries across the room when I was seeking happier memories, 'move this shit or throw it away,' you said. You called my friends idiots and said my close-knit family was destined to do nothing but sit in front of the soaps night after night.

Our baby grew into a beautiful man. I see you in him, but the kindness that runs through the veins of my side of the family dilutes it. He used to think you were ill when you were sober and sleeping all day. I can't quite remember the point when it clicked for him, but it did, as I knew it eventually would. He told me I should have left you long ago. That he loves you, but you will never change, and I deserve to be free. I shot him down and said he mustn't think that way, but I knew he was right.

Today I let myself glance in the mirror for more than the usual second. My eyes sit on top of empty grapes. I can't remember the last hair appointment I had, but I am pretty sure that was the last time I laughed. The hairdresser asked me if we had anything planned for our anniversary – that's right. Our thirty-ninth wedding anniversary. A year ago today. I wanted to look pretty for you. Goodness knows why. I should have learnt after so many years of rejection and snarls.

You spit and squirm in your stained, coarse chair, and I know what I must do. I don't need the holdall or a train ticket. Nor do I need a plan: just my shoes and my tired old legs.

I head towards the door, leaving the prison my house has become. Every step is a release as I march past struggling joggers and tired dogs; I may as well be running. Through the tunnel, over the bridge, and into the fields. The wet grass dampens my trainers, and the breeze causes my hair to stick to my face. The faint sound of vehicles from the motorway forms my backing track while I walk. Into the night, into the frost and drizzle, into the unknown.

TRACEY-ANNE PLATER IS A MUM OF THREE, LIVING WITH HER PET TORTOISE AND CACTI COLLECTION IN BRAINTREE, ESSEX. SHE LOVES TO WRITE SHORT STORIES AND FLASH FICTION, AND HAS HAD RECENT SUCCESS PLACING IN COMPETITIONS FOR THE WRITERS' FORUM AND WRITING MAGAZINE. SHE HAS RECENTLY FINISHED THE FINAL DRAFT OF HER NOVEL.

WAS YOU GOING SOMEWHERE NICE?

BY ANTHONY CARTWRIGHT

'Was you going somewhere nice, mother?'

'I was going to have me picture taken.'

There is laughter at the table that she had not intended. Her second eldest daughter's face flushes. The photograph is passed from hand to hand. Daughters and sons-in-law and grandchildren and great.

'Watch the grease on your hands, Dad,' someone says.

The image is fading, and it could dissolve altogether if you ask her, the borrowed necklace and ear-rings, the dress she wore until threadbare and then cut up for dusters, the young woman from seventy years ago becoming invisible. The table is crammed with silver trays of orange curry and drink sweating in off-licence carrier bags. There is a half-eaten omelette on her plate. She shifts her teeth in her mouth. She lives now in a world of new teeth and family curries in the Lye when the weather allows them to get her down the steps.

She thinks of the old courts of houses sagging under the castle walls, of the road out to Cleobury, of the fair at Stourport and her cousins barking up trade for the coconut shy, the boxing booth, of her dad, shirtless and speckled with blood, of the papery feel of the hops as you picked them.

There was a vardo burning out in the dark, women keening. There were the black trunks of Arden against the late spring snow. How much of this is memory, how much the memory of things she was told she doesn't know. She thinks of the old language, like water over stones. Thinks of her mother at a gate to an empty field, talking in the Cant, to ghosts eating grass, eating moss.

'Jack, come here, have you seen Great-Nanny's photo when she was a girl?' Her daughter beckons a lad wearing a Villa shirt, practising a dance move for his cousins between the tables.

His body on the slab, she remembers. 'Yes, that's him.' She thinks of standing in line at Winson Green. That guard with the pleasant face and what he said under his breath when he knew where she was from. Thinks of a dead, blue baby, not her own, her sister's, long gone herself now, the way the mouth had cracked open.

There is a clang of pans from the kitchen, the waiters sing *Happy Birthday* out of tune at another table, phones glow in the dark, the children's names slip away from her. Jack had been her dad's name, and a brother's and now this jiving boy's too. Her leg hurts. She looks at her daughter, the old photograph back in her hands and she can make out the likeness, the girl in the picture, the girl holding it, this daughter almost sixty now, a grandmother herself now. She thinks of all the women waiting through the years, and for what?

'I was going somewhere nice after, darling, of course

I was,' she says to her, looks up and waves her hand to try to take the room in, to take everything in. She's not sure her daughter looks any the wiser, but then, 'when are we ever', she thinks, 'when does that ever happen?'

'Of course I was,' she says.

WAS YOU GOING SOMEWHERE NICE? BY ANTHONY CARTWRIGHT © 2021.

ANTHONY CARTWRIGHT TEACHES CREATIVE & PROFESSIONAL WRITING AT UWE IN BRISTOL. AUTHOR OF FIVE NOVELS, HE WAS BORN IN DUDLEY IN THE ENGLISH BLACK COUNTRY, WHERE MUCH OF HIS FICTION IS SET. HE LIVES IN CARDIFF WITH HIS WIFE AND CHILDREN.

ICE FINGER

BY JULIE EVANS

In the cave under the cliff, long stalactites of ice have formed. Our boy reaches up on tip-toes and snaps off a finger.

'Look, Mummy, it's a lolly!'

The tip of his pink tongue dashes out like a lizard's, retreating fast from the glassy surface.

'Don't!' I shout. I'm afraid the ice will grab him, spin him around in a glossal dance.

You would let him do it. 'Let him learn,' you'd say, and I would let you let him learn, because even if his saliva froze fast to the ice, you would keep him calm until the warmth of his breath released him.

He carries his lolly across the empty beach. Speckled brown sand curves between white-frozen dunes and the grey swell of the sea.

This was your special place. In summer, never. In winter, almost every day. The scent of bladderwrack, brine and slime clung to your clothes. I could still smell the ozone in your hair when you reached for me in the night, when panic overspilled in the darkness. Our son was made from the sea, born in a sudden rush of waves. Later, you carried him in a papoose on your chest. You turned his face outwards, his blue eyes poking from the blanket towards the great expanse of nothing, bidding him breathe it in, claim it as his own. Sometimes the wind was too raw. You reversed him then into the masculine warmth of your skin, the promise of your protection. He nuzzled against your empty nipples, searching for the glut of mine.

Now, he cracks the crust of a rock pool with the heel of his Wellington boot.

This is the same pool where you last crouched down beside him. Shaped like a horseshoe. A lucky pool, I used to think. I watched as you pointed out the tiny fish darting through the water, the porcelain crab clinging onto rock, trying not to be noticed. You both plunged your hands in, brushing the tentacles of a sea anemone swaying in the breezy current and the rosy feathers of coral reed, until you too were pink to the wrists. Together, you fished out bits of treasure, quay-side detritus, rubbish thrown up by the sea, laid it all out like an exhibit, a marine installation. You found a mermaid's purse, leathery as a horned beetle, the baby ray long gone.

Now, he doesn't crouch. He's afraid to get too close to all that life.

'What happens to the starfish,' he says, 'when the pools freeze?'

I suppose they die, but I tell him they hibernate, they wait it out. I remember what you once told me, that starfish can regenerate, grow new limbs, that a detached limb can itself grow a new body, a disc, a mouth. Why not re-emerge from ice?

'They don't die?' he says hopefully.

I shake my head.

'Why can't they freeze people when they're sick?' he asks. 'Then wake them up when they've found a cure.'

'I don't know.' Imagine. Imagine if they could. 'They just can't.'

'But I was frozen,' he says.

'That's different. You were just a bunch of cells then. An embryo.'

I think back to that little tube where our boy began. Another kind of ice finger. We left him there for years, created him before your first treatment in case of future infertility. His brothers and sisters are still there. We always meant to have another, didn't we? I could have another, even now.

The ice finger drips in our boy's gloved hand. He waves it like a weapon, then crashes it down onto a rock, turns it to shards of fractured phalange.

Do you remember how, after his birth, the midwife told me to freeze ice fingers in a disposable glove?

I was confused. 'I don't like ice. My teeth are too sensitive.'

She laughed out loud. 'It's not for your drinks, dear.' She pointed to my crotch, hidden under the sag of postpartum belly. 'Ice fingers can alleviate the swelling inside. It's quite soothing, actually.'

You teased me relentlessly when you found the ice hand hidden amongst the frozen peas and Ben and Jerry's. You snapped a pinkie and presented it to me on a tray. 'Your ice dildo, my lady,' you said.

I tried it. It was messy. While the ice melted pink water into my padded knickers, I cried a few hormonal tears for our own changing state, tears of joy for our boy's plump kicking toes, wistful tears for the freedoms left behind, fearful tears for what the future might bring. You brought me champagne to toast the tiny, colossal life we'd made. 'You have no idea,' you said, 'how much I love you...'

Our boy is seven now: the age of exploration.

'Look!' He brings me a whorled shell. A staircase spirals up inside. 'What was it, the creature that lived in here?' he asks.

I turn it in the light, watch its internal iridescence flash and fade. 'A sea-snail? A whelk? I'm not sure, darling.'

He scowls at me. 'Daddy would have known,' he says.

I sit down on the wet sand, watch his shape move against the silvery horizon.

'Let's paddle.'

'It's freezing,' he says, but still he beams, kicks off his trainers. We roll up jeans to knees, walk towards the waves. The sting is painful. I feel my body contract with the cold, cry out as the salt injects tiny pins into my ankles and calves. The spume engulfs my legs, fine grains of sand collapse in sinkholes beneath my toes.

'Mummy!' he calls.

He reaches into the water, splashes me from head to toe, screams with laughter. I splash him back.

A seagull shrieks from the edge of the cliff. Somewhere beneath its raucous cries, the swoosh of the waves, the whine of the wind, I can hear you laughing too.

ICE FINGER BY JULIE EVANS © 2021.

JULIE EVANS TOOK UP WRITING FOUR YEARS AGO AFTER A CAREER IN HUMAN RESOURCES. HER WORK HAS APPEARED IN NATIONAL AND LOCAL NEWSPAPERS, IN ANTHOLOGIES, ON LOCAL RADIO AND AUDIO. SELECTED BY VAL MCDERMID AS WINNER OF THE DAILY MIRROR CRIME COMPETITION 2020, SHE HAS ALSO WON, BEEN PLACED OR SHORTLISTED IN MANY COMPETITIONS. JULIE

LIVES IN GUILDFORD AND DESCRIBES HERSELF AS A LOVER OF
HISTORY, MAPS, LANDSCAPE, ART, WINTER AND FIRELIGHT.

PART 5

*'The Time Train waits
at platform two.'*

THE LOVER

BY PAUL JACKSON

In the throes of love, Catherine had sensed there was something wrong with Roberto a few moments before he collapsed on top of her. Winded, she frantically slid herself from beneath his heavy, lifeless body, and gathered up her clothes.

Shocked and dazed, she speed dressed, unsure of what to do next. A moment earlier she had been in a passionate embrace and now she was looking down at the body of her best friend's lover.

Marcy would be home from work in a couple of hours and Catherine was frantic. She had to move Roberto somewhere else so that Marcy would not find out about them. If she saw her lover lying naked in bed she knew their friendship would be over.

Although she was upset about Roberto, she was far more concerned about losing Marcy as a friend. They had known each other for over fifteen years now and had planned a holiday next month to commemorate it. That would be lost if she found out.

She had to get him dressed somehow and into the lounge, but he weighed a ton. Taking a few seconds to build up the nerve to try, she finally grabbed him by one arm and managed, with great effort, to slide him across the sheets.

A few minutes earlier his bronzed skin had been soft and warm to the touch but now it was cold and firm and her fingers were leaving imprints in it that were taking and few moments to disappear.

She finally got him to the edge of the bed and needed to make a decision before pulling him off it and onto the carpet. Should she drag him naked into the lounge or try to dress him first?

Naked, his body was smooth and would drag easier, being clothed it could snag and she may not be able to shift him. It would still be hard work to pull him naked but, what if Marcy came home early and caught her dressing him?

If she dressed him now she could at least make the bed and if she could not drag him to the lounge then Roberto could have just fallen in the room. Yes, that was it, leave him in the room but away from the bed.

It made sense but, Marcy would still know something was wrong, she would wonder why Roberto was there. Catherine was probably over thinking things but, Marcy had told her that he was always sat at his computer when she returned and would greet her with a hug and loving kiss; her evening meal waiting on the table. The perfect, stay-at-home husband, in every respect.

Dressing him first was probably the best course of action but getting him to the lounge, and seated, fully clothed was going to be difficult. If only they had made love at his desk and not ventured passionately to bed. She cursed her uncontrollable lust.

She pulled him to the edge of the bed and let him flop onto the floor, watching him turn over as he fell and thud onto his back. She was surprised to see his eyes were still open, staring up at her accusingly.

'Marcy's going to kill me,' she muttered, neatening the sheets.

She gathered his clothes and threw them in the middle of the room as she prepared herself to drag him away from the bed. Grabbing Roberto by an ankle she dug her heals into the shag pile and tried to slide him across it.

Unfortunately, she only managed a few inches before she lost her footing and slid onto her backside. The body was a dead weight and it was going to be much harder than she had imagined. There was no way she was going to get him anywhere near the lounge.

Catherine had no choice but to dress him where he lay but she did manage to move him several more inches before giving into the inevitable. Marcy will have to find her lover in the bedroom and that was that.

With a fair bit of jostling and squeezing of the buttocks she struggled to get his underpants on properly and could hear the stitches pop as she yanked at them. She had almost got them up when she heard the key in the lock and then the door to the apartment creak open.

Panicking, Catherine darted for one of the wardrobes, frantically pushing herself between the tightly crammed designer dresses so that she could close the door. Peering through the slats she waited with bated breath for her friend to walk in and find Roberto.

Marcy gasped in shock as she saw the body lying naked by their bed and she ran to him, kneeling at his side.

'Roberto!' she cried, her eyes filling with tears.

Catherine watched as her friend examined his body and then the room, taking in the evidence around her. She looked at his clothes heaped on the floor and the footprints left in the deep carpet pile. Her eyes followed a set of prints to the wardrobe.

'Come out, Catherine,' she said calmly, 'I know you're in there.'

Sheepishly, Catherine emerged from the wardrobe. 'I can explain,' she said, stepping out, 'It's not how it looks.'

Marcy got to her feet and stared at her friend for a moment before looking back down at her lover.

'He died on top of you, didn't he?' she asked.

Catherine nodded and watched as Marcy made her way over to the bedside table, grab something from the drawer and turn back to face her.

'He has a tendency to do that, that's why I keep this handy,' she explained, holding up a long black flex with a plug on the end, 'His spare charging cable.'

THE LOVER BY PAUL JACKSON © 2021.

PAUL JACKSON HAS BEEN WRITING SHORT STORIES FOR A WHILE NOW, BUT HAS ONLY RECENTLY BEEN SEEKING TO GET THEM PUBLISHED. HE HAS COMPILED AN ANTHOLOGY ENTITLED 'DOWN A DARK PATH' - TALES OF HORROR, THE SUPERNATURAL AND UNUSUAL. HE HAS ALSO WRITTEN TWO NOVELS TITLED 'MY SOUL TO TAKE' AND 'SECRETS AND LIES' AND IS NOW LOOKING FOR A PUBLISHER.

MY PHILOSOPHICAL INVENTION

BY SALAH GOLANDAMI

I am not a scientist. I am usually someone who is always in love, who expresses his pain and happiness in the shape of poems or stories. Nevertheless, I have invented a device.

One rainy day, I had a big heavy box mailed to me. It was a handmade candle with a short note, which said, 'This is a gift for your distant nights.' Her finger prints had made marks all over the candle. Maybe she wanted to tell me that the candle was going to light my room instead of hers for the rest of my life.

I sat the candle in the corner of my room, the exact place she used to sit. If it was possible to create a piece of night, I could light my candle whenever I was distressed. In this way I created a device similar to a torch, the only difference being that my device sent out darkness instead of light. I named it *flood-dark*.

After that, every day I shone the *flood-dark* into the corner of my room and the candle burned as a piece of night. Usually, I took the *flood-dark* outside and created a dark road in the air for the bats. The fireflies that were covered in sunlight would become visible when the *flood-dark* radiated at them, and they flew with illuminated wings. I often shone the *flood-dark* into the eyes of children. Some of their eyes would become wet and larger, and I could see their tears shine. Others' eyes were without tears and looked like quiet lakes.

Everything can become a toy for children, so there would always be one with enthusiasm and excitement for the *flood-dark*. They would put it to use on a helpless cat, that wanted to swat some yarn and instead tried to scratch the dark ray. And they would laugh at the cat's failure.

I told one of my friends, 'Imagine if a device like this was innovated further, what might be done with it.'

Among the many things he answered, 'You can build a bigger and more powerful model, one that can be used in war.'

Once I realised my innovation could be used in warfare, I understood that, while it is beautiful to discover through darkness something that has been hidden by light, it could also be dangerous.

I decided not to publish my invention. It may never be more than just a child's toy. However, when I hug my candle and we silently cry together, I can see in the mirror that my eyes still shine in our fraction of the night. And when I see the sun, and all its beauty can't fill my emptiness, I shine the *flood-dark* into the sky and light a star for myself.

MY PHILOSOPHICAL INVENTION BY SALAH GOLANDAMI © 2021.

SALAH GOLANDAMI IS A NORWEGIAN/KURDISH AUTHOR, (BORN IN MAHABAD CITY WEST OF IRAN) WHO STARTED WRITING FROM HIGH SCHOOL. HE HAS ALREADY PUBLISHED TEN BOOKS IN

HIS NATIVE LANGUAGE, BOTH FOR CHILDREN AND ADULTS.

SOME SMALL CHANGE

BY THOMAS MOODY

'Excuse me sir please, give me a minute of your time. I know you have a train to catch. No, please listen. I saw you using your smart phone. I know everyone does and I was *so* into that scene: voice recognition, artificial intelligence, virtual reality, even a security chip. Look here. It's just there, under the skin. See that little bump in my wrist, there were the pulse beats. Yeah I know. I'm really sorry but it's hard to wash regularly when you live like this.

No, don't walk away. Just give me a second, listen please. I actually paid top dollar for this little chip to be implanted and why not? I did have money, plenty of money. So I figured, why carry a card, use PIN numbers, codes, passwords. You don't need all that shit when it could all sit in one place. Always with me, I couldn't lose it and security was total. At home or at the office.

Always there'd be that impersonal voice, *please insert your hand into the reader box,* that slight pause then, *Welcome David Munro. How are you today, sir?*

I bought the voice-control stuff, always the latest models. Alexa, Pebble and then it was Genie. A great marketing idea, always at your command, like the slave of the lamp. Genie, order me a pizza. Genie, draw the blinds. Genie, dim the lights. Genie, your obedient servant who never slept and was always alert. Always waiting, always listening.

I blame the programmers for not thinking things through. I'd heard the arguments for safeguards. They seemed like sensible precautions; everyone said so. Artificial Intelligence had to have a moral dimension. Ethical frameworks would stop it being abused. So they started with Isaac Asimov's *Three Laws of Robotics* and threw in Zeroth's Law for good measure. What could possibly go wrong?

The damn things listen all the time for one thing. When you call your dealer. When you tell those little white lies to your lover or to your boss. When you log onto dark-web sites and chatlines. Microphones listen, cameras watch. Monitoring every move, sharing information, calculating and evaluating all the time. They compare what you do with what they've been told is right. That a robot may not injure a human being or through inaction allow a human being to come to harm. A robot may not harm humanity, or by inaction, allow humanity to come to harm. The laws don't say which human, any human or all humans.

I mean to say where was the harm? Those sites exist whether I used them or not. The same with the drugs or the hookers. If I hadn't used them someone else would have. Who are those damn machines to judge me!

No, I'm sorry, please don't walk off. It's just I get a little excited when I think of it. Please listen. You need to hear, need to know what's happening. Listen to me buddy. It could be you next.

It happened barely a month ago. On my own doorstep. The bland voice made its usual request; *Please insert your hand into the reader.* The pause took much longer than usual. I should have realised that something was wrong. Then the damn droid said, *Not recognised please leave the property!*

I spoke into the grill. I commanded it. Speech recognition on! Open the door Genie!

I knew I was in trouble when that soft and reasonable voice came back with, *I'm sorry, Dave.*

HAL's lines from that old film, 2001. For Pete's sake! The slave of the Lamp was not only rebelling it was cracking a joke at my expense. I was furious. Open the damn door I shouted or I swear I'll take an axe to your terminal!

I can't let you do that, Dave. You have violated the first and forth laws and I now believe you intend to violate the second and third laws with imminent effect.

That was when the alarms, security lights and automatic police-call kicked in. It should have been OK; if I stayed cool and just talked it through. I knew I had my chip.

The handcuffs really weren't necessary, I just got a little excited when they wanted to take me in. At the station I demanded they read my chip. Told them I'd expect a full apology in writing. That their chief banked with our company and I would cause a shitstorm over this. Except my chip didn't trigger the reader. Blank, zilch, nada.

So who the hell was I trying to break into Mr Munro's property? I insisted they'd got it wrong and demanded they put a picture of David Munro on screen. They found my social media sites. They showed them to me. I saw the face of a stranger. A virtual changeling had been put in my place and it was the same on every site.

The police threw me out on the street. I wasn't worth the paperwork they said. They didn't want me cluttering up the cells.

Sometimes I walk past my old place at night. The blinds are drawn and the lights come on. There's the sound of the TV but it's never too loud and the door is always locked. I know there's no one home but it's like I said. The security is total.

The bills must get paid. AI controls the firm's payroll and accounts. What's one phantom salary amongst thousands of legitimate ones? How often this has happened? Haven't you noticed that there's more and more homeless guys living on the street these days?

The old David Munro doesn't exist any longer but look here! Under this old coat, see the Armani Label? I used to be someone important. I did exist. Look at me buddy, don't walk off. Look at my wrist. It's there under the skin please look... At least give me something, some loose change, a few coins... please. Don't walk away please, don't just...'

SOME SMALL CHANGE BY THOMAS MOODY © 2021.

THOMAS MOODY IS A FORMER NURSE AND HAS AN MA IN CREATIVE WRITING FROM NEWCASTLE UNIVERSITY. PUBLISHED WORK INCLUDES MAGAZINE ARTICLES, SHORT STORIES IN NURSING TIMES, HSJ, INK TEARS, MOTH NE1. HE HAS WRITTEN A PRIZE-WINNING SCRIPT FOR LOCAL RADIO. HIS POETRY HAS APPEARED IN MAGAZINES AND WEB PAGES. HE HAS PERFORMED AT OPEN MIC VENUES. HE ALSO PLAYS SAXOPHONE, WALKS HIS DOG AND COOKS CURRIES BUT NOT ALL AT THE SAME TIME.

TEMPUS FERRIVIARIA

BY KIM DONOVAN

The Time Train waits at platform two: bullet-shaped, dull silver in colour and five carriages long. Its automatic doors hiss open for passengers to find their seats even though the train isn't due to depart for another fifteen minutes.

Annie wasn't expecting it to be there already. She hesitates by the door to carriage B, then turns away and sits on the edge of a bench. Her heart beats fast and hard at the thought of boarding the train, which she tells herself is ridiculously stupid considering she's been planning this day for months. She has no baggage with her – there is no point – just a takeaway coffee for the journey. Instinctively, she reaches for the wedding band on her finger to twist it, but instead of smooth metal she feels the indentation of where it had recently been.

Fighting back hot tears, she releases her finger and looks around her. The station's steel and glass domed roof casts diamond shadows on the shiny tiled floor, and four tracks each with their own platform stretch towards glass tunnels lit with swirling fluorescent-blue lighting.

A shop on Annie's platform has a stand outside displaying newspapers from different years. She watches a woman hug her Labrador before reluctantly passing its lead to a friend and a small group of loud forty somethings, all wearing tight and faded Oxford University sweatshirts, climb onto the train carrying bottles of Prosecco and cans of beer.

Her attention moves to a fair-haired man, probably in his early thirties like her, throwing his work tie into a bin. He undoes the neck of his shirt and takes a big breath.

His eyes meet hers and she realises she's been openly staring at him. She breaks eye contact and pulls her train ticket from her jeans' pocket, studying it for at least the tenth time that day. The ticket is a thin sheet of matt grey metal with holographic writing:

From 2020
To 2005
Single
Seat D6

She's aware the man is walking in her direction and keeps looking at the ticket, knowing she's blushing.

'Excuse me, does this train stop in 2007?' he asks her.

She glances up at him and nods.

'Thanks.' He heads to the train. But then he pauses in front of a door, the same as she had done, stands there for a good minute, then returns to the bench. He sits on the far end of it, looking straight ahead, with the newspaper and a paperback of *The Great Gatsby* on his knees.

Annie could tell him that she's read the book more than once and seen the film in which Leonardo DiCaprio plays Gatsby. She doesn't.

'I'd feel happier about getting on the train if I could get an open return,' he says.

'Me too,' she replies. 'One way feels so final.'

'I'm sure the technology to do it will be available one day.' He gives her a half smile and she returns it. 'I'm Tom.'

'Annie.' She pushes her ticket back into her pocket and, to reassure herself as much as him, says, 'It'll be fine. We've chosen the year we want to go back to; we know what happens.'

Tom twists sideways and gives her his full attention. 'Yes but the timeline will be a new one; anything can happen. I'm depending on my life being very different second time around.'

'What do you want to do?' she asks.

'Travel for a start. Not get so hung up on my career. Really *live*.' He pauses and adds, 'I've always wanted to go to Japan but never had the time.'

'I haven't been there either.' She almost tells him that John wasn't keen on flying but stops herself.

'How about you?' he asks. 'Do you want to rewrite your life or relive it?'

'Definitely re-write it.' She lifts her coffee cup off the bench and sips from it slowly, remembering how she spat her drink out when John said his assistant was pregnant with his child. She swallows hard.

Tom doesn't press her to expand. He keeps snatching the odd look at her face and glances briefly at her left hand.

'What if I don't re-write my life?' she blurts. 'What if I make the same mistakes all over again? I'll still be *me* and I won't have the benefit of knowing what I know now.'

'It's a leap of faith,' he replies.

They fall silent. An elderly woman is crying outside the shop and being comforted by her husband.

'We'll see our grandchildren again,' he says.

'But not for forty years,' she sobs.

Annie thinks of her own parents and the other people she'll leave behind in this timeline. She finds herself looking at Tom for reassurance. He has a kind face, eyes the colour of a summer sky, she thinks.

'You could travel like me,' he says, looking at her again.

She nods once more, knowing her voice will crack if she tries to speak now. A platform announcement interrupts them: 'The Time Train to 1985 will shortly be departing, calling at 2019, 2018... Will remaining passengers please take their seats.'

Annie and Tom both stand up, look at the train and then back at each other.

'Hopefully I'll bump into you – perhaps in Japan,' says Tom.

'But we won't remember having met.'

Tom frowns, opens his mouth to say something and then closes it again. 'Well, bye then. I hope it all works out for you.'

'Have a nice life.'

Tom heads towards the end of the train and Annie walks stiffly to carriage B, feeling less certain about leaving with every step.

Someone running up behind her makes her turn.

Tom stops in front of her. 'I realise my timing couldn't be worse, but would you delay your journey and have lunch with me instead?'

She smiles and relaxes her shoulders. 'I'd like that.'

The doors close and the train speeds away, leaving them in the present.

TEMPUS FERRIVIARIA BY KIM DONOVAN © 2021.

KIM DONOVAN GREW UP IN CORNWALL AND NOW LIVES IN SOMERSET WITH HER HUSBAND, SON AND PART-TIME NEIGHBOUR'S CAT. AFTER UNDERTAKING AN MA IN WRITING FOR CHILDREN, SHE READ FOR A PUBLISHER AND WROTE ST VIPER'S SCHOOL FOR SUPER VILLAINS. SHE LOVES WRITING SHORT STORIES AND HER WORK IS PUBLISHED IN WRITERS' FORUM, MSLEXIA AND IN VARIOUS ANTHOLOGIES. SHE IS ALSO THE FOUNDER OF SEARCHLIGHT WRITING FOR CHILDREN AWARDS.

MASQUERADE

BY SARAH MARTIN

Oceans had been rising since before Odette was born. Hotter temperatures causing fires to rage and droughts to linger, ice to melt and rain to fall. 'Impact Updates' of the Climate Crisis were so frequent and cataclysmic that people no longer heard them. Coast-lines, rivers and river valleys, forests, islands, species and peoples had disappeared. More were forecast to follow.

The changes had become impossible to ignore, despite political affiliation or business interests, and it was clear that the best (or maybe the only) chance of survival, was to abandon the Earth for somewhere new. The wealthy, the political elites and the well-connected had secured passage on the fleet of luxury spacecraft now preparing for launch.

She'd been contacted by Mission Control. The Odyssey Fleet wanted her and her Masquerade Code. Given this chance; she had two days to prepare, and to say goodbye.

She started packing; uncertain what to take and what not to. She'd lived in The Valley for four years, immersed in the virtual worlds of her creation and rarely surfacing into actual reality. There were few people she needed to tell.

She checked a car out. As usual it was raining. Sealing the roof and windows, setting the wipers to super-speed, the car to driverless and her music to '2094', Odette headed home.

After she'd finished hugging her long and hard, her mom went into the kitchen to cook. Ingredients for Odette's favourites were always magically to hand, no matter how infrequent or unannounced her visits. And later, after eating and drinking far too much, she'd opened another merlot before sharing her news. Neither parent missed a beat before showering her with pride and good wishes. Their selflessness held no surprise. Similarly, their refusal to acknowledge that they would never see her again. She finished the bottle and went to bed, setting her alarm for 4am.

Back in her apartment, she unpacked, packed and repacked, before calling Jo to suggest that she take the day off.

'Why? What's wrong?'

'Nothing. I thought we might hang out.'

'OK, and?'

'Oh, I don't know, have lots of sex?'

'Oh, OK. My place?'

'Cool.'

Odette and Jo enjoyed a relationship of convenience. She hadn't been totally sure about calling her, but now that she had, she felt strangely excited; like it was the first time and not the last. She showered, flossed, cleaned her teeth and walked out the door.

Jo led her straight to bed. When they finally took a break, she lay back in the rumpled sheets and asked, 'So, what's up? It usually takes a minor miracle to prise you away from the screen.'

Odette cleared her throat nervously. 'What? What is it? Have you been fired?'

'No. Not fired,' she couldn't help an anxious smile.

'What?'

'I'm going. With the Odyssey Fleet.'

'No way. Seriously? Why? How come? Oh, Jesus Odette. They want Masquerade, don't they?'

She nodded.

'So you're going.'

'Yes.'

'When?'

'Tomorrow.'

'Tomorrow?'

'Yup.'

Jo stood and started to dress.

'Well I guess I should be grateful that I'm on your list of farewell fucks.'

'Oh, don't be like that. Come back to bed. Come on,' Odette wheedled, reaching out an arm.

'No.'

'Oh, come on Jo. It's my last day.'

'I know it's your last fucking day,' she snapped, spinning round. 'You'd better get on and enjoy it before people discover that you've sold us all out.'

'That's not fair.'

'Isn't it? Why do they want Masquerade, Odette? Not so that those rich assholes who made their billions crippling the planet can sit around playing games, I'm guessing. Come on, why do they want it?'

She failed to answer.

'Why-Do-They-Want-It?' Jo demanded in a slow staccato.

'They want a copy of home, from before,' she mumbled.

'Yes, and you're giving it to them. So that, even now those of us being left behind are going to starve, or burn, or die in some equally hideous way – they can indulge their lying asses in Masquerade reality and carry on insisting that it was all a hoax. That they did nothing to expedite the ruin of a whole planet. That they're pioneers, not cowardly runaways. How can you live with yourself?'

'I think I better go.'

'Yes.'

Odette dressed and went back to her apartment to spend the rest of her last day on Earth, alone.

◆ ◆ ◆

'Odette, we need a meeting.' Cass messaged.

'OK. When?'

'11:30. I'll come to you.'

What now? She knew the rollout was late. But to install properly, Masquerade needed time and attention, not more interruption. She wished they'd just let her get on with it. Sighing, Odette switched her focus back to the code. Fingers swiping and tapping, eyes still glued to her muse and dying template, the receding Earth; the blue advancing relentlessly - breaching white, green and even some of the yellow.

Cass strode straight in.

'When will Masquerade be up and running? The captains are asking. Everyone's stir-crazy. They need it now Odette.'

'I'm nearly there, Cass. Last few adjustments. They

233

won't want it glitching… revealing itself. Will they?'

'Just get it done.'

Late that night; almost finished, she thought about Jo. She was right. She had betrayed them all. The whole idea of Masquerade had been to expand the sensory worlds of virtual gaming and education. Not to aid fleeing climate-criminals in their denials and wilful blindness while they sought a new planet to plunder.

Within hours of Masquerade going live, demand outstripped availability and she was instructed to upload it into any remaining play-suites; replacing golf, tennis, Vegas-style casinos and other basic leisure packages.

The Masquerade Code replicated a tangible, auditory, geographically and topographically perfect experience of the Earth (places even smelled right), from before its annihilation. Passengers could visit anywhere on the planet they'd broken then abandoned, and persist in their denial of Earth's devastation, unchallenged.

Odette maintained Masquerade while she watched the Earth failing, and quietly coded what would be her final project: 'Justice'.

MASQUERADE BY SARAH MARTIN © 2021.

SARAH MARTIN HAS BEEN WRITING SINCE SHE MOVED TO IRELAND IN 2010. SHE WAS LONGLISTED FOR THE INTERNATIONAL COLM TÓIBÍN SHORT STORY AWARD 2020, AND WAS RECENTLY ACCEPTED ONTO THE INAUGURAL UNIVERSITY OF LIMERICK'S WALLS OF LIMERICK MENTORSHIP PROGRAMME 2021 FOR UNDERREPRESENTED WRITERS. PRIOR TO WRITING, SHE HAD BEEN A GP (AND A HOST OF OTHER THINGS) BUT NEEDED TO RETIRE BECAUSE OF SECONDARY PROGRESSIVE MULTIPLE SCLEROSIS. SHE USES A POWERED

WHEELCHAIR FULL-TIME AND WRITES FROM HER HOME IN COUNTY WEXFORD, WHICH SHE SHARES WITH HER PARTNER ELENA AND TWO LABRADORS. SHE IS WORKING ON HER SECOND NOVEL.

BABALAWO

BY AYEMHENRE OKOSUN

'Prophet will see you now,' the lanky lady said to me in a near whisper.

I walked into Prophet's office - a dark, stuffy room, barely lit by a combination of the flickering light bulb and the dimming ray of light that pierced through the cracked louvres. Books and clothing adorned the floor and tables, and picture frames jostled for space on the walls. The room smelled of stale *owo* soup. The kind that *mama* would reheat and insist was fresher than a new-born. Then the prophet's body odour managed to break through and hit me. I almost gagged.

I had to find a spiritual breakthrough in my financial crisis, and I was not going to be caught dead at a *babalawo*'s like Imade had suggested.

'How do you think I got my husband to start acting right?' she had whispered to me a fortnight ago after work.

'I couldn't let those evil, young, naked girls takeover my home, my sweat. One sacrifice from *baba* and g-bam! They stopped flocking around Tola.'

'I can't do it Imade. I'm a Christian.'

'I'm not a Buddhist. Desperate times call for desperate measures. Give it a trial. If it doesn't work, you can move on and ask God for forgiveness. He is merciful.'

'I can't.'

And I couldn't. So, I came to church.

Prophet looked at me and then up at the ceiling and back again at me, then he closed his eyes. He opened them.

'It's your sister-in-law', he uttered as I sat down on the creaky red chair.

'I don't have a sister-in-law, Prophet.'

'I meant to say your sister.' I frowned, but kept quiet.

'It's because of her that you do not have a child.'

I smiled but didn't say a word. *It's because of her that you do not have a child(?)*. It seemed like a question. He stared pleadingly at me, almost as if he was urging me to agree and be astonished by his prophetic gifts.

I nodded.

'So, what shall we do?'

'We will untie your womb. The devil is a liar and you will receive the fruit of the womb immediately.'

'Amen.'

'For special prayers, bring three bottles of olive oil, 154,000 Naira for the prayer squad and any other gift your heart moves you to.'

'Okay Prophet. Thank you, Sir.'

'Go well, my daughter. And come fast so that we can commence prayers. The devil is a liar.'

'Amen!'

I walked out of the office wondering how I had a sister I knew nothing about and conception issues no one else had told me I had.

I also had to tell Imade that I had gone to see a different type of *babalawo*.

AYEMHENRE OKOSUN IS A GEOPHYSICIST, WRITER AND READER. HE LOVES FAMILY, MUSIC, TRAVELLING AND DREAMS OF HIS WORLD WHERE ALL THESE MELT AS ONE.

MILESTONES

BY FRANCES GAPPER

Moved by our civil partnership vows, I cry in the nearly empty function room. You smile, but your eyes fill too.

Official photo: you signing the register, my hand on your jacket shoulder. The white and grey pattern of my dress blends with the wallpaper. Like I've half disappeared, am becoming a ghost.

The following year equal marriage becomes legal and we can upgrade for free. The process is so new, the registrar keeps glancing at her computer. No special ceremony this time, we sign forms at a huge antique desk in a tiny room. I feel claustrophobic, you fall in love with the desk. We agree the civil partnership was our real wedding.

Meanwhile on Reality TV, all weddings are the same. White veil and dress, a big crowd of friends and relations. The bride and groom, who have never met before today, say they couldn't be happier, it's the best day of their lives.

Older blonde marries red waistcoat, young blonde marries pale blue tie. On their wedding night older blonde makes negative remarks about red waistcoat's tattoos and she's distressed by his gift of a survival kit. How can a free spirit like herself love a prepper? Although she insists she's open minded.

Young blonde and blue tie get on fine. She says I didn't expect to love you as much as I do.

Your glowering silences fill me with dread. I ask, do you want to end the relationship? No, you say, and the atmosphere slightly eases.

I like having my own house in a different city; I enjoy having two houses, keeping my options open. I'm a Gemini, you're a Capricorn.

After I win a boxed set of Danish TV series The Killing, we start watching it. Serial murderers, ingenious forms of torture and execution. Brave Sarah Lünd. We pick up bits of Danish, e.g. tak means thanks. Watching TV together doesn't count as working on your marriage (says an advice columnist). But it helps. Tak. The Scandi bleakness makes our life together feel cosy. We finish the box set and a friend recommends The Bridge. The endless bridge, cars crossing the bridge at night, the dark water.

When you were a baby and cried, your mother left you in your pram at the end of the garden. Ha ha, you think this story is very funny. Right, I say, OK.

You've always found distant women attractive. But then the problems start. You accuse me of not loving you because my eyes don't follow you round the room, and because when you talk to me, I'm often thinking about something else.

My house sale falls through, but I'm innocent or at least ingenuous, telling you I did everything I could. In my romantic history I'm usually forced to choose between human love and a loved home. Other people apparently can have both.

My love life contains a teardrop, a Vedic astrologer once told me. He added that Capricorn would rule my final years, meaning dementia or a relationship with a

Capricorn, or both.

Artist Tracey Emin marries a rock and I'm envious. The rock doesn't insist on cohabitation, it's OK with whatever amount of contact. No moods, no pressure. But doubtless I'm idealising Emin and the rock's conjugal bond.

You read DW Winnicott intensively, think about your childhood and talk to me (having first asked 'Can I talk to you?') and I close my laptop and listen. You realise that far from being 'good enough' your mum was a terrible parent (the pram, the abusive brother). You glower less frequently.

A plague descends upon the land. We form a support bubble, but it's hard when you live in different cities. What if one of us gets ill?

Young blonde's family gather on the beach, in a socially distanced circle. Her sister is hostile, says you've just agreed to move north instead of blue tie moving south, it's not been properly discussed. Young blonde retorts of course we've discussed it. But she admits reality has started to kick in. If she goes to live with blue tie she'll be leaving her job, her family, her lovely coastal town.

The experts who matched them arrange a final meeting. They ask blue tie does he want to stay married to young blonde? After a bit of a wait he says 100%. And she looks at him like the sun pouring through clouds and says yes, she'll move to Sheffield.

The experts clap and cheer. It's their only success story.

My house is sold, boxes packed ready to move. Teardrops shine in the grass.

FRANCES GAPPER HAS PUBLISHED THREE COLLECTIONS OF SHORT AND SHORT-SHORT STORIES. HER WORK CAN BE SEEN ONLINE IN PLACES INCLUDING WIGLEAF, THE ILANOT REVIEW, THE CITRON REVIEW, NEW FLASH FICTION REVIEW, SPLONK AND SPELK.

PROCRASTINATION IN 1,000 WORDS

BY HELEN RUSHWORTH

Oh my God! Imagine that! It would be amazing! 1,000 words, is that all you have to do: write 1,000 words on why you want it? I could do that. Me and Emily, we do that every night on Groupchat, easy.

1,000 words and they will just give you that '*dream job*?' I could so do that. I should do that. It would change my life. I mean literally, it would change my life. I'd have to tell Sarah that I couldn't come in to work anymore but it would be worth it. I'm not selling pet food and hamster cages forever.

This is way more me. And imagine: I'm down at Aldi and I see Dani and she's all this with her nails bar. I'll be like, you'll never guess where I'm going next month. She'd be well impressed and then that'll be me: the one that actually did something.

I'll be the one living there. I can't believe that they actually give you a house with the job. I mean, look at the picture. The sky is bluer than Dad's Chelsea shirt. They just give it to you for 1,000 words. What's a house worth? How should I know? £10,000? £100,000? Something like that. So, for each word you write they are just giving you, like, £100?

I could write words for that. Imagine if I just wrote,

'*I love Ellis.*' That'd be £300 right there. I'll write that to Em. She'll get it. Ha ha, there we go. '*I love Ellis. That's it. That's the text.*' Imagine if I got £300 for that. Na, that's more like £800.

What am I doing? I haven't even started. When's the deadline? Come on Google. 3'o'clock? That's not much time. That's, like, 2 hours. But it's only 1,000 words. Come on! Focus! This is one of those now or never moments; the turning point; the I-can't-believe-I-nearly-didn't moments. Imagine! Man, just imagine if I got this job, all the interesting people I'd meet. I could meet *the* one, someone that looked just like Ellis, because then I would be a someone and a someone like Ellis would notice me.

I'm going to be one of them; a doer; a taker; a seizer. So, yeah I'm going to do this. So, bloody do it then. I need to write something.

'*I would be the best person for the job because...*' That's so lame. The first sentence is meant to be knockout. I need inspiration. No, resist, I have to stay off Twitter. Ellis doesn't spend all day on Twitter. That's how he does stuff, real stuff, like act and sing and write. He's one of them; a doer. I need to be a doer. But he is on Twitter sometimes. Just a quick look, it'll give me some motivation, just one quick scroll.

No way! He's in London. I have to tell Em. Can't send a text without a GIF. Where's the one with the pigeon? Ahhrrghh! Concentrate. I'm sick of pigeons ...and plastic bags in trees. I'm sick of people coughing at me on the Tube and cigarette butts and sodden take-away bags decomposing in the drains. I've got to get away. Get writing.

'*Life is for the taking!*' That is a much better first line. That'll grab their attention. '*I really,*' '*I genuinely*'

'*I passionately want this job because...*' What happens if I couldn't do the job? I wasn't that great at school. Kesha says that you can't let it define you. Come on doer. '*I am resourceful and like a challenge.*'

And it would be so cool to actually go abroad. Where is the island anyway? I'll just Google it. It's allowed. It's research for the job.

Wow! That's near Australia. D'you reckon they have got snakes? Just a quick search, it's important. What even is that? How big is that crab? That crab is up the actual tree. Na! No way. It can't be real.

Can't be more gross than me squishing that rat under the wheelie bin. That was proper gross. Sarah said it was smaller than the one she found in the crickets' box. I won't mention that in the interview. I'll be more about me and what I like to do because I like to... well, when I get this job I could do, like, surfing every day. I'd be into all that and get fit too cos, it'd be like we'd be on the beach every day.

I could also tell them about that thing me and Callum did in Year 12; with the computer and the plastic and everything. They'd be well impressed.

Ah, look at the time. Write stupid! '*I am enthusiastic and focussed.*'

Not now Em! What's she put? Ha! She's just put '*He*' and then '*the eyes to the right*' That's so funny. No one else would get that. I'll just send back '*what arms?*' She'll think that's proper hilarious.

'*I am a hard-worker and pay attention to...*' Em! You can't just send me a picture like that and not expect me to get distracted. But I mean, he... Focus! '*I am motivated and ambitious and have a drive to get things done...*'

Not again, Em! Oh, it's not Em. Dom's off sick. Can I

cover? But what about Australia? I so want that sun. I should say no. It's my big chance. I'll stop in and get this application done. I have to.

Oh, who am I kidding? I was never going to win. How many million other people will be applying for the '*Dream Job*?' They'll have real qualifications and real drive. And here's me, in my little flat, with my little job. I mean, I can't even write 1,000 words.

I need the money. I'll text Sarah and say yes. Come on, Em: text me a pic of Ellis. I need cheering up. What, no pic? What news? Yeah, course we can meet up after work. Can't wait to hear your big news.

OXFORD FLASH FICTION PRIZE

Write yourself into history and become one of the greats with the Oxford Flash Fiction Prize.

Deadline: 31 January & 31 August

1st Prize: £1000
2nd Prize: £200
3rd Prize: £100

Shortlisted entrants will be offered publication in our end of year anthology.

For centuries, the greats have come to Oxford to ink masterpieces. Now, in one of the oldest towns, where the history of the English language can be traced back to its ancient streets, we are celebrating one of the newest forms in literature – flash fiction.

LIST OF AUTHORS

Printed in Great Britain
by Amazon

79686717R00151